A STEAMY ALIEN MONSTER ROMANCE
ENSLAVING EZMIRA

LEANN RYANS | V.T. BONDS
USA Today Bestselling Authors

Copyright © 2021 Leann Ryans and V.T. Bonds

Cover design by Getcovers.com.

All rights reserved.

No part of this book may be reproduced in any form or by any electronic or mechanical means, including information storage and retrieval systems, without written permission from the author, except for the use of brief quotations in a book review.

***

For more books by Leann Ryans in a variety of worlds, check out https://leannryans.com.

***

Go to https://vtbonds.com for a complete list of books by V.T. Bonds.

For new releases, discounts, and Knotty Exclusives, subscribe to V.T. Bonds' newsletter at

https://vtbonds.com/newslettersubscriber.

Contents

Chapter 1 9
Chapter 2 19
Chapter 3 31
Chapter 4 41
Chapter 5 47
Chapter 6 57
Chapter 7 65
Chapter 8 75
Chapter 9 87
Chapter 10 93
Chapter 11 105
Chapter 12 115
Chapter 13 119
Chapter 14 125
Chapter 15 135
Chapter 16 145
Chapter 17 155
Chapter 18 165
Chapter 19 177
Chapter 20 187
Chapter 21 193

Chapter 22	205
Epilogue	221
Author's Note	227
Unknown Omega by V.T. Bonds (Preview)	231
Monster's Find by Leann Ryans (Preview)	237
Rescued and Ruined by V.T. Bonds (Preview)	245
Tempting A Knight by Leann Ryans (Preview)	253
Follow V.T. Bonds	259
Follow Leann Ryans	263

Chapter 1

Ezmira

The applause jolted Ezmira out of the spell she'd fallen under. Blinking, she relaxed her muscles as heat warmed her cheeks. No matter how many times she performed, it always surprised her when people enjoyed it.

Pasting on a smile, she drifted her gaze across the people in the ballroom, not focusing on any one person, but trying to make each attendee feel seen and included. It was a trick her troupe mates had taught her long ago, yet this time a person standing by the stage caught her eye. A large alpha stared directly at her, standing out because he was the only one not clapping. He looked like some of the other attendees in his military uniform, yet where they had proud wings folded behind them, he had nothing. His shoulders hunched forward, and despite the pinched expression around his eyes, a tingle of interest skated down her spine.

Pulling her attention away from the male as her flush deepened, Ezmira turned and slipped backstage. She'd never been one to seek attention, and the emotions she'd battled lately left her uncomfortable when she couldn't escape into her dance.

The dimness behind the heavy brocade curtain brought a sigh to her lips, her body drooping as the last of her energy rushed away. She loved to dance, but it'd become more draining as time plodded on. She'd once thought she could live off the energy of the crowd, but as life slowly wore her down, she grew to need more.

Whatever more may be, she didn't know.

"Great job, Ezmira. As always."

A large hand dropped onto her shoulder, a quick kiss pressing to the side of her head before Jolie moved on to put his instrument away. She flashed a brief smile he likely didn't see. Unnamable emotions curled in her gut. Jolie was open with his affections, showing her the same friendly touches he did everyone else, despite the way she always held herself apart. She couldn't let anyone get too close. Every time they did, catastrophe ensued.

Swallowing the lump threatening to choke her, Ezmira looked around for her shoes. She reserved the ones on her feet for dancing only, since she didn't want to risk scuffing them or wearing out the sole any faster than necessary. A good portion of her pay went toward her performance footwear, and there was no reason not to care for them like the expensive items they were.

The others of her troupe moved around her, putting away their instruments and changing clothes. It was a familiar routine, one that happened after every performance, and was soothing in its normalcy despite the other emotions roiling beneath her skin.

The majordomo stepped into their space, clearing his throat to draw everyone's attention.

"You all did a wonderful job. Please accept our appreciation and honor us by staying and enjoying the festivities."

With his announcement made, he turned and disappeared.

Ezmira glanced around at the others, noting the excited looks and quiet whispers. She wanted nothing more than to return to their hotel, but she wouldn't make the rest of the troupe miss this opportunity because of her. They always showed up and left together, so she couldn't head back to the hotel alone. Mingling with the type of people attending the coronation ball could land them another performance that would cover their costs for far longer than when they performed on the next planet's streets for spare credits.

Pushing away the mixed emotions coursing through her, she stowed her dancing shoes inside their trunk. Some members slipped back out to join the audience, but despite the rumble in her belly and the knowledge that there was food on the other side of the curtain, she couldn't force herself back out into the light.

"Are you okay, Ez?"

Ezmira turned at the light touch on her arm to see Selena looking up at her with wide eyes. Because of her omega nature, Ezmira was on the small side, but Selena was a Sylph and even tinier than her.

"Yeah, I'm fine. I think I just need a breather."

Selena smiled, giving her a nod before slipping around her. Not wanting to be in the way or appear to be lurking, Ezmira looked around for somewhere she could unwind, but the area backstage was filling with the next performers and people packed the ballroom from wall to wall.

Hands trembling, her chest heaved with growing panic until she spotted the open doors to her left. The darkness of the night sky beyond was all the convincing she needed to make her escape. Darting from the safety behind the curtain, she wound past the few people standing between her and her goal, each step closer to freedom loosening the tight band around her chest.

Slipping through the door, she heaved a sigh until the sight before her caused her breath to catch. Flowers of every shape and color danced in the gentle breeze perfumed with their scents, fountains adding a tinkling background that drew her forward despite the weariness in her bones. She spotted little statues and benches nestled between bushes, and while she could hear soft voices scattered through the darkness, it was far better than the press of bodies inside.

Following the sounds of water, Ezmira let her feet carry her further into the gardens, the bushes enclosing them letting her imagine she was in her own world, far away from the demands that weighed her down.

As much as she loved to dance, the constant travel was wearing on her, leaving her feeling disconnected from everything. Each week brought a new planet, a new city, a new venue, a new audience, only to be replaced with another the following week. The only constant in her life was the people she performed with, yet even they sometimes changed. The novelty had long worn off, and the urge to settle somewhere was growing, yet her troupe relied on her as their main performer. Guilt plagued her every time she thought of trying to find a place she could make a home.

Sucking in a deep breath, she tried to let the thoughts go, focusing on the faint music drifting to her on the wind. When she stepped out into a clearing containing a small waterfall splashing over a pile of rocks, she realized she'd reached the farthest corner of the gardens. On the other side of the small stream and iron fence was pure blackness, the surrounding forest's massive trees creating a canopy so thick the moonlight couldn't shine through.

Shoulders drooping, Ezmira sank to the ground beside the water, dipping her hand into the coldness. A new song reached her ears, bringing a smile to her face as the image of watching her mother dance to it filled her head. Swaying, she let her eyes drift closed, soaking in the peace she'd found, even though she knew she'd have to leave it.

It wasn't long before she was humming the tune under her breath, her muscles twitching with the need to follow the steps. Eyes still shut, she rose to her feet, letting the sound of the water and the rustle of leaves paint a picture of the space in her mind. She moved slowly, letting her body follow the melody as her feet glided over the earth. The tiredness she'd felt melted away, her spirit lifting for the first time in years.

The snap of a branch and a sudden rumble caused her to stumble, eyes flying open as her head turned to the sound. Her body responded to the noise before she could register what it was, belly cramping as her instincts screamed to submit.

A dark form separated from the shadows near a wall of bushes, her heart leaping into her throat as she shuffled backward. The hunched shape moved closer, and while her mouth opened, no sound emerged as she watched the looming form grow larger. Another harsh sound poured from the thing before her, causing her to stumble again and freeze in place lest she fall and lose the ability to flee.

Monsters didn't exist. They didn't creep out of the darkness and growl at you when you were trying to recover from the drain of giving your soul to a room full of people for the hundredth night in a row. She had to be mistaken.

"H-hello?"

The shadow stopped moving toward her, but there was no response. Trying to work some moisture into her mouth to speak, she straightened her back and tried to get the fear under control.

"Are you lost? C-can I help you?"

There was more silence before the figure in front of her moved again. The small bit of light from a nearby lantern finally fell on the shadowy shape, revealing a massive male staring back at her, but he didn't look right. With his shoulders hunched and the skin around his eyes and mouth pinched, his expression was just as scary as the unknown had been.

"Perhaps."

The deep rasp of his voice sent a shiver down her spine, causing Ezmira to wrap her arms around herself. The wind shifted, bringing her the scent of alpha male soured with the stench of pain. It was enough to make her realize he was the male who'd stared at her and stood as still as a statue while everyone else clapped at the end of her last performance. She tried to hide her trembling, pulling herself up taller and hoping he couldn't tell her dynamic. It had been stupid to wander off alone in a strange place, but she'd thought the palace grounds would be safe.

Swallowing thickly, her tongue darted out to wet her lips before she spoke again.

"Am I in the wrong place? I'm sorry if I am. I'll leave."

Pausing for a moment, she sucked in a deep breath to steady herself before taking a step to the side to move around the male. Another harsh growl forced her muscles to seize, fear sending her pulse thundering through her veins. A shameful trickle of dampness soaked her panties, her body unable to ignore an alpha's call.

"No."

The rough word caused her trembling to worsen, her breath to stutter, and her mind struggled to think of what to do. Should she call out for help? Should she run?

"I'm sorry," she whispered again.

She hadn't realized she was crying until the breeze blew over the wetness on her cheeks, chilling them and sending another shiver through her body.

The sudden sound of male voices broke through the quiet outside the clearing, and hope sparked for a moment before the words became clear.

"I saw the little dancer go this way. She was alone."

The male before her turned toward the voices, but she saw him shift back to face her. His shoulders seemed to sag lower before he straightened himself and took a step closer.

"So am I, but don't worry. I'll take care of you."

His movements seemed to be in slow motion as he reached for her, but her muscles refused to respond to her commands to flee. All she could do was watch the hand coming for her and pray her troupe could move on when they realized she was gone.

Chapter 2

Quasim

Quasim knew he shouldn't have taken her, but for the first time in forever, he hadn't been able to deny himself. The words of the males pursuing her were enough to prompt him into action—he couldn't leave her in danger. The situation warranted that he take her, even if she balked.

Her terrified expression fed his self-hatred, so even though his intention had been to touch her vibrant green locks of hair to see if they really were as soft as they looked, he'd been furious by the time his hand cleared the distance between them. She'd been foolish by putting herself in danger, and even more so to expect him to leave her there.

Her mouth opened as though to scream, and the sounds of the men getting closer forced his hand.

He dug his fingers into the well of her shoulder, clamping the nerve against her collarbone.

She crumpled.

He caught her under her arms before she fell out of reach, the sudden movement stealing a hiss of pain from him.

After a ragged breath to regain his senses, he marveled at her delicate features and lithe body. Even as limp as a rag doll, she exuded grace unlike anyone he'd ever met, and she was light as a feather.

She must be an angel who fell through a rainbow.

It took no effort for him to envision a halo resting on the tiny, fuzzy antlers peeking out from her shimmery green hair. No one without divine powers could dance with her passion and suck his pain away.

His memories reared their ugly heads, giving him visions of gleaming metal and red-hot iron, followed by searing agony and evil voices. If it weren't for his brothers' support, he never would have made it out of the enemy's hands alive, and the pain was a daily reminder that he hadn't let the enemy win.

Realizing his fingers dug into delicate flesh, Quasim forced his nightmares aside and lifted the gorgeous omega. He didn't have a plan. He just knew he needed the peace she gave him as she danced.

After settling her face-down over his left shoulder, he ignored the pull of mangled flesh as her slight weight draped down his back. It took a moment of tiny shifts before her dangling shoulder no longer brushed against the stump where his wing once protruded, but eventually he secured her.

He'd only meant to watch her from the shadows, much as he had in the ballroom during her performance, but without the cloying press of the crowd, he'd gotten lost in her scent.

He needed her.

***

Scowling around the corner and scanning the darkened doorways lining the crumbling cobbled street, he deemed the way clear and stalked to the other end.

When he'd first moved to Cryptik, a city deserted over a century ago, he'd never planned to have an omega. The streets were dangerous in the best of times, but with a sweet-smelling little female like the one draped over his shoulder, his chances of finding trouble grew exponentially as he traveled from his ship to the place he called home.

Especially with her bright, colorful clothes fluttering in the breeze. He felt stifled by her long, flowy skirt as it escaped the grip he had on her legs and flapped in his face. She turned an inadvisable situation into an outright deadly mission.

It was worth it.

When the had music played and her body moved, his pain disappeared. The agony in his soul drifted away, carried by her grace and raw emotions, and for a while, he forgot how wretched his life had become.

He didn't care how ridiculous he sounded. It only took watching her sway to the first few notes for him to know she held something no medicine could ever give him. Pain was a living thing he would carry for the rest of his life, alongside the memories of what had happened, and even a moment's relief was worth any price.

Stopping beside the dilapidated entrance to the building of his carefully crafted sanctuary, he tilted his head and cursed his predicament.

He'd draped his prize over his left shoulder, since it was the stronger of the two, but the burns and scars on his head rendered him nearly deaf in his left ear.

Her breasts shifted against his ribs, alerting him to her steady breaths and easing his worry.

She'd have a headache when she woke, but he'd take care of her so she could dance away his agony. She'd have no choice.

A quick scan of his surroundings confirmed they had no stalkers, so he ducked into the building and clambered up the first few flights of stairs with his normal, annoying limp.

By the time he got to the fifth level, his right leg burned, the twisted ligaments in his knee threatening to give out with every step. He gritted his teeth and forced his leg to carry him upward, unwilling to risk losing his prize because of his weakness.

Halfway up the seventh staircase, he paused and gathered his will. After a few deep breaths, he shifted the tiny omega closer to his neck and crouched down, growling in pain as her torso brushed the stump denoting his absent wing.

A quick shift ensured his talons wouldn't get stuck in the warped wood before he darted forward and up, clamping his arm tighter around his stolen trophy as he launched himself over the void. Air rushed past his face, causing bittersweet memories of his life before his enemies destroyed his body to flit into view.

Grunting as his scarred hand connected with the wooden beam several feet away, he clamped his talons around it and hoisted himself upward, demanding his screaming muscles cooperate. It was tricky, hard work shuffling between wood and stone, but he pivoted his body to the outside of the building and wove his way up the remaining floors.

He'd chiseled divots in the ornate carvings, creating a meandering path up and around the trellises warped by decay. From the ground, his path was invisible, and the buildings on the other side of the street weren't as tall as his, so if anyone were watching from the windows, they couldn't see how to get to the first few feet of handholds.

His gut clenched when a gust of wind threatened to rip him from the decrepit gargoyle hanging under his favorite perch, but he snarled his annoyance and swung himself over the railing. When he landed, his entire body rebelled at the jarring impact, the tiny female over his shoulder sending streaks of agony from his mangled stump into his spine.

She'd make it better tomorrow as soon as she began dancing.

He stalked across the balcony and went straight to his bedchamber, where he pulled her over his shoulder and slid her onto his bed.

His sheets would smell like her.

Perfect.

No. Not perfect. She would dance for him. Nothing more.

Yet he couldn't stop his gnarled finger from tracing the beauty of her dark cheekbone.

Snarling at his stupidity, he hobbled to the chest near the hallway door and retrieved a length of chain.

After winding it around the bedpost, through the design, and connecting one end to itself, he brushed her colorful skirt up her leg.

Her slim ankle tempted him, the memory of her feet carrying her across the dance floor easing the torment in his soul. Resisting made him angry, but he avoided touching her flesh as he closed the ring of metal around her ankle.

With a grimace as the scars on his wrist pulled his flesh and reminded him of the darkest days of his life, he snapped the lock shut.

His heart died long ago, when cruel enemies slowly burned and cut away pieces of his body. He had no light left. There was nothing but hard hatred and miserable agony left in his life.

Except now he had a beacon. An escape.

And she was so soft.

He sighed in exasperation and forced himself to stop stroking her hair. Despite the tangles from her prolonged trip upside down, she was still heart-wrenchingly beautiful with her ebony skin, delicate features, and plump curves.

Since she wasn't awake to relieve him of his suffering, he turned toward the hallway door and closed it before engaging the myriad of locks he'd installed. She wouldn't be able to reach the top three bolts, if his calculations were correct, but it didn't matter. He'd make sure she never had the chance to reach the door.

Locked in the safest place he'd ever found, he turned to face his bedchamber and assessed the space. There wasn't enough empty floor for her to dance here.

It wasn't anywhere near as big as the ballroom, but the main room connected to his balcony would suffice. She'd have more square footage than the stage if she danced in there, but he couldn't secure it like his bedchamber, so they'd have to return here every evening before the sun set.

The tiny bundle of color resting on his bed made him aware of how drab his sanctuary looked. His scowl tugged the scars on his face and ear, souring his mood further.

There wasn't a safer place in the entire city. Safety mattered, not color.

He'd have to guard his heart around the eclectically dressed woman. Already her influence on his soul threatened to warp his tentative hold on reality. Nothing mattered except surviving one day to the next to prove he was more than the assholes who'd stolen his wings.

Since his new form of medicine was unable to perform while unconscious, he hobbled to the adjacent room, making sure the thick curtain covered every centimeter of the archway before flicking the switch on the water heater and cranking the pump until water gurgled out of the hose. It splashed into the massive tub as he rose to his full height and fumbled through unbuttoning the ridiculous ceremonial vest he'd worn to his friend's coronation ball.

Armyn was more than a friend. They'd grown up together, joined the military together, even fought in a war together. Armyn was one of a very select few he called brothers, even though none of them were blood related.

Without Armyn's ruthless wit, he never would have found the will to continue once he'd returned to his homeland broken and useless.

Reminding himself of this, he suffered through peeling off the fancy layers of clothing and hung them up in the storage bags. Once free of the stifling fabric, he pushed everything to the back of the clothes enclave and limped back to the tub.

Sinking into the steaming water, he swallowed down vomit as his muscles spasmed so hard he almost cried out. With no one to witness his misery, he let the horrific pain flow through his expression. After a few moments of sitting in the hot water, the cramping eased enough for him to draw in a full breath.

The mottled scars surrounding his demolished back felt as though they'd split open in the scorching water until the warmth sunk deep enough to loosen the tissues and allow him slight relief. He glanced at the stars through the broken window, but turned his face to the ceiling before his yearning grew.

He'd never fly again.

Tilting backward so his entire back submerged under the water, he reached over and turned off the hose. After soaking for a few minutes, he braced himself on the lip of the bath and rose to his knees before standing. Not wanting to drain the water after just one use, he flicked the power to the water heater off and yanked the drain lever down so it would stay closed as he stepped from the bath.

Unable to pace his room naked to dry like normal, he stood dripping over the drain in the middle of the floor before pulling on trousers and finding a clean shirt. It was threadbare but held the lingering scent of soap, so he carefully lowered it over his head and threaded his arms through the holes.

Gritting his teeth as the material settled over his deformed back, he tugged it down his torso and settled it on his hips.

To hell with it. He wouldn't torture himself just because an omega occupied his den.

He tore the shirt down the middle, taking it off as quickly as he could and tossing it to the floor of the clothes enclave. The pants followed, his knee screaming as he lifted it to yank his talons free of the thick cloth. He'd bought them for the coldest part of winter but doubted he'd wear them. The fabric was too stiff, too rough to rest against his sensitive flesh.

He grabbed his favorite pair of pants and slid them on.

There was a rip from when he'd been relearning how to dress himself and his spasming talon had caught the fabric, but he couldn't bring himself to part with them.

They signified his life. Broken but still forced to exist.

Pushing the curtain aside, he found his prized omega still asleep. With the sun not due to rise for a few more hours, he decided he would skip his normal nightly pacing altogether so she could rest.

He wanted to see her, even if she wasn't dancing.

After lighting two candles and placing them on the mantel, he ignored the call of her softness and sat in the corner chair, knowing it would obscure him from her sight when she woke. The medication hidden on the other side of the room called to him, but it would dull his senses too much, and he refused to take it.

For now, he'd make do with the soft rise and fall of her chest, the even cadence mimicking the rhythm of a song older than words.

When she woke, she'd dance for him.

Chapter 3

Ezmira

Ezmira's brow furrowed, the pounding in her skull causing her to wince. Raising a hand to her head, she tried to remember what had made her pulse throb through her cranium. When nothing immediately came to mind, she cautiously opened her eyes.

The ceiling above her was interesting. Shadows twisted across it, dancing with the flickering light that had to be coming from candles. She could tell it had once been a beautiful mural, but those days were long past. The image was dull, riddled with cracks and a few missing chunks that appeared to have fallen free of their home. Despite the apparent neglect, it still held her attention, a strange feeling of kinship growing in her chest with the decrepit masterpiece.

The tension in her head eased, so she lifted it to look around. She didn't recognize the room, but no alarm speared through her since it was rare for her troupe to spend more than a day or two in one location. The past few years had been a long string of unrecognizable rooms.

Ezmira couldn't help the groan that escaped her as she pushed up onto her elbows to get a better look. Her troupe wasn't rich, so disrepair was something she was familiar with, but this room appeared worse than usual. The walls were a grungy color somewhere between cream and brown; the one to her left sported blackened veins from a leak in the roof. There was an unlit fireplace across from her with smoke stains on the mantel where two flickering candles sat, and other than a trunk against the wall on her left and a low dresser on the other side of the mantel, there was little else she could see.

Pushing her mass of emerald hair behind her shoulders and trying to detangle it from her antlers, she sat up, but when she tried to cross her legs, one wouldn't move. Frown marring her face, she reached out to loosen whatever held her but was shocked to find smooth metal.

Her startled voice came out in a whisper. "What?"

Leaning forward, she grabbed the chain with both hands, mind working to figure out what was going on. The padlock holding the chain about her ankle showed this was no accident.

Heartbeat fluttering in her throat, her breaths came short and rough as she yanked on the chain, twisting the lock in a vain hope it would come free. Pulling her leg did nothing but dig the warm metal into her skin, but the growing need to fight and get away wouldn't allow her to stop.

Following the chain to its other end, she found it wrapped around the thick wooden bedpost, a loop going through part of the ornate design on the footboard to prevent pulling the chain up and over the top, which was way above her head. Mind growing fuzzy, a sound in the furthest corner of the room drew her attention. The light didn't quite reach there, and it was only the motion that caused her to realize what was lurking.

The memory of the garden returned in a rush, her gasp sounding loud in the silence between them. Tugging harder at the chain, she realized the scent on the bedding was the same as the male who had apparently taken her captive, and instinct took over.

Rolling onto her belly, Ezmira crawled as far across the bed as she could, a whimper escaping when the chain scraped the skin of her ankle and stopped her. She had enough slack to sit on the farthest edge from the scary alpha, but unless she jumped over the footboard or moved to the side closest to him, she couldn't reach the ground.

"Where am I?"

Her voice came out slightly hysterical, but she felt like that was appropriate considering the situation. When he didn't answer, she gave the chain another tug and let out an inarticulate cry.

"Where have you taken me?"

More silence met her question, and she couldn't stop the hiccuped sob that broke free of her chest. She knew why an alpha would take an omega like her, but the question slipped past her lips anyway.

"What are you going to do to me?"

Her whisper was pitiful, causing her to cringe and struggle to control her reactions. She was alive. That was the important part. If she could keep herself focused, she could escape.

"Calm yourself."

His deep rumble filled the space, causing her heart to clench even as she barked a laugh.

"Yes. Calm is the rational response to kidnapping and—and whatever else you plan to do to me."

The hiccup in the middle and sniffle at the end ruined the sarcasm she was going for. More tears trickled down her cheeks, but she refused to give in and accept what she thought was coming. She would stay strong through whatever happened.

"Nothing will happen to you. I'll keep you safe. I only want you to dance for me."

Ezmira eyed the shadow with disbelief.

"Most people who want me to dance for them offer to hire the troupe, not kidnap them."

"Not them. *You*."

She huffed, turning away from the corner. Her eyes searched for something to use as a weapon if he came closer. She couldn't believe the male didn't want more. He was an alpha, after all.

"Still," she muttered. "This is not the way to go about it."

Motion at the corner of her eye snapped her attention back to where the male sat. Dull orange claws flexed in the candlelight, causing her eyes to narrow. Many of the ball attendees had feet like that since they'd been in the Raptyr capital, but the male hadn't had wings. Even as dark as it was in the garden, wings weren't something he could hide, and her view of him in the ballroom had been clear.

"There were men coming, so I had to protect you. I didn't have the time to discuss payments or ask questions about your services, and I doubt you would have agreed anyway."

The bitter note at the end caused her to frown. Despite the fear, she couldn't help her growing curiosity about her captor. She'd yet to see him clearly since glancing at him in the ballroom, and while there was a lingering pain and acrid tinge to his scent, it was still that of a virile alpha male. They weren't usually the type to feel lacking.

Trying to think of a way to coax him into the light, her eyes moved to the fireplace. There was a chill in the air that she hadn't noticed through her panic, but the longer she was still, the more the cold crept in. A light blanket covered the bed she sat on, and the mattress was thin and lumpy and definitely not capable of offering much protection from the elements.

"Well, I can't dance half frozen."

She wrapped her arms around herself to emphasize the point. She knew from the few alphas she'd associated with that they ran hot, and he wasn't likely to realize she was exaggerating. The chill *would* make her muscles stiff, but she doubted it would matter anyway.

She waited through the silence, eyes locked on the bulky shadow filling the corner. When he finally moved, she held her breath, not sure what she expected to step into the light. Her mind was still screaming about monsters. Whatever she'd expected, it wasn't what she saw.

The male was definitely a Raptyr. His torn pants left little of his physique to the imagination.

The clawed feet connected to sturdy calves, climbing higher to strong thighs meant to launch him skyward. Although he hunched forward instead of standing proudly. But the low-slung waist revealed a powerful, muscled body, and while she couldn't help the bloom of warmth inside her, the sight of the scars pulled a gasp from her chest.

Every Raptyr she'd ever seen had small, downy feathers covering their entire body. One evening, after performing in a small tavern, she'd gotten to touch a female Raptyr's arm, and had marveled at how soft the plumage was. From a distance, Raptyrs looked to have smooth skin since the feathers were so tiny, but this alpha who'd captured her appeared to be missing almost as much of the teal down as he had left. Many of the feathers stood up around puckered scars that crisscrossed every bit of visible skin on his arms and torso. There were broad swaths where there were no feathers at all, the scarring so bad it didn't allow them to grow back, exposing the darker turquoise skin beneath the slightly lighter feathers.

He paused at her sound of distress, dark eyes narrowed in a glare. The scar bisecting his cheek would have given him a grim countenance even with a smile, but the snarl pulling back his lips elevated him to the level of a nightmare.

Hands curled into the blanket beneath her, Ezmira trembled as he stalked closer. She couldn't pull her gaze from his, an odd mingling of fear and something shameful flooding her veins. This was a male who knew pain intimately. He'd survived something horrible and life altering but didn't cower. It was natural for her body to respond to his dominance, but it was still embarrassing in the situation.

He finally freed her from his hypnotic control when he turned to the fireplace, kneeling to stack wood from the pile on the side of the hearth into the space. The new angle gave her a view of the worst of his wounds, and her heart clenched in sympathy for his loss. Tears spilled from her eyes as her hands rose to cover her mouth and muffle the cry that wanted to escape.

Where his wings once sprouted from his back, now nothing but two raw stumps rose. Ropes of angry scar tissue surrounded the base of the bone she swore she could see peeking from the flesh. The entirety of his back looked as if someone had flayed him for days. The black ends of the stumps must be from when they'd cauterized the wound to prevent blood loss.

They were the worst injuries she'd ever seen, in both physical and psychological aspects.

To take any flighted being, sentient or not, and remove their wings from them had to be the vilest act possible. It was a wonder the man still lived after so much trauma, and her anger at his surliness lessened.

Swallowing against the bile rising in the back of her throat, Ezmira turned her eyes away, trying to steady her nerves against what she must do. Injured or not, the male had taken her against her will, and she had to do whatever she could to escape.

Scooting toward the opposite side of the bed where she'd be able to reach the floor, she searched again for something to use as a weapon. Even a chunk of stone from the walls would have worked, but the only thing she could find was a thin pipe lying next to the baseboard. With no other options at hand, she went while she had the chance.

Moving with a silent grace born from her years of dancing, she sprinted across the floor to reach for the pipe, but she'd miscalculated the length of her chain. Stopping short with a sudden jerk, a startled cry spilled from her lips as she pitched forward, palms and knees making painful acquaintance with the floor. Casting a frightened glance over her shoulder, certain he'd heard her, she stretched her hand toward the pipe, triumph flooding her as her fingers curled around the cold metal.

Chapter 4

Quasim

Really?

She knew her cuff kept her chained to the bed, and yet she tried to run?

Quasim dropped the wood to the floor and stood, slower and steadier than he could have without the adrenaline pumping through his veins. The slight sound of her frantic lunge across the room kicked up his predatory instincts, making him wish he could spread his wings and frighten her with their impressive span.

He threw the useless urge away and used the flare of fury at his loss to turn ever so menacingly toward her.

His theatrics went unnoticed. Her back faced him while she stretched toward the wall.

The snarl he released startled her. The hunching of her shoulders sent a flick of intrigue to his base instincts, even as something foul twinged in his chest.

He pushed it out with a growl.

One enormous step changed his angle enough to see her hand. She tugged at the airflow pipe, her entire body jerking with the effort.

"Having trouble?"

She froze.

He waited a heartbeat.

She yanked with a frenzy born of panic until the pipe he'd stooped over for three days while he rebuilt his sanctuary gave a tiny squeak before wiggling.

Fury coalesced with his adrenaline, carrying him across the room. His uneven gait thudded against the floorboards as he descended on his prize.

Her curls filled his fist before she gave another tug. Terrified green eyes met his, but her slender fingers remained tight around the pipe. He reached down and grabbed the link of chain closest to her ankle cuff and snarled as agony speared through his back, the odd position tweaking mangled muscles, tendons, and flesh.

He yanked and stood, ripping her away from the pipe by her ankle and hair so fast she landed on the bed before her squeak escaped her lips. After releasing her, he checked the pipe for lasting damage before turning and going to the chest on the other side of the room.

Her startled inhale pulled another snarl from him. She had no reason to be surprised he'd stopped her, but if she was going to be unreasonable, he'd find a shorter chain.

He froze.

What would a shorter chain prove?

His past had taught him anything could be a weapon. If she were resourceful, she could easily fashion a shiv or lock pick from the materials surrounding the bed.

Her whimper mingled with his furious growl as she stayed exactly where he'd tossed her, staring at him in fear.

He slammed the trunk closed and fastened the latch, twisting the dials to lock the ancient thing—as he should have done the moment he brought her into the room instead of waiting for her to act so foolishly—before stalking the few steps to the little round table next to the chair he'd been in when she woke. When the drawer opened with a grinding sound, he grimaced, then plucked out the set of keys resting at the front.

He'd have to find a new hiding place if she didn't show a bit of reason once faced with the truth of her predicament. Somewhere high might work, but it would be a tricky balance. Sometimes his right arm refused to raise above his shoulder, the thick scar tissue and seized muscles limiting his reach if he strained it. Like he had when he carried her up the building.

He palmed the circle of keys, letting the sharp ridges dig into his hand before turning to face the bed. She shrunk under his stare, her pupils dilating to contrast with brilliant green irises. When he stepped toward her, she shifted away from him, rekindling his need to chase despite having already caught her.

As a gust of wind battered the outside of the building, the section of airflow pipe she'd pulled on rattled. His brows lowered, adding a pinch of discomfort from his burned scalp to the myriad of pain shooting through his body. He dropped the keys back onto the table and stomped to the trunk. After unlocking it, he rummaged through it until he found what he wanted.

His joints creaked as he stood.

She shifted on the bed, earning another growl. He shot her another glare, wishing she were dancing so he could escape the agony coursing along his nerves.

He filled the space between the pipe and wall with the glue he'd extracted from the trunk before dropping the lid closed again. The lock engaged as he spun the dials to random numbers.

When he turned to retrieve the keys from the desk, her colorful slipper caught his attention. Her delicate feet made him yearn to see her grace in action. He had no clue what he'd do if she refused. It wasn't an option.

His scowl deepened as he noticed the reddened flesh above her ankle, where his impulsive toss had pulled the cuff into her leg. He hadn't broken skin, but he shouldn't have risked hurting her fragile limb.

He'd limit his touch to her hair from now on, unless she required stricter guidance.

The stench of acrid fear filled the space between them. He used it to wipe away the lascivious thoughts creeping around the edges of his mind. No omega would want his attention, so just the threat of his nearness should be enough to deter her from making more rash decisions.

He turned toward the table but felt her eyes watching him as he picked up the keys.

No doubt his wounds disgusted her. They disgusted him. He couldn't bring himself to look at his scars, yet he forced her to stare at them since they were on full display. His past ruled him. Every miserable second he'd fought to live, each tiny victory of supposed recovery, meant he'd bested his enemies and proved them unsuccessful, but he'd never be of any true worth. His mangled body attested to that.

He may not deserve it, but he'd found relief in her dancing and he'd do anything to keep it within reach.

Turning to her, he pointed to the pipe before speaking.

"Don't destroy things you can't fix. You could have suffocated us or caused a fire."

She trembled as he stalked toward her, the bare floorboards doing nothing to soften his irregular gait.

"The chain is for your protection."

After a beat of utter stillness, her fear took a backseat to a myriad of other emotions. He stepped closer, enjoying the way her nose scrunched and her lips tightened.

Another step brought him to the foot of the bed.

"How is stealing my freedom protecting me?"

She braced as he leaned over her.

Chapter 5

Ezmira

Her heart lurched into her throat when he took her ankle in his hand again. Imagining the worst was an automatic reaction, but when he reached for the lock, her breath stilled.

Was he letting her go?

She pulled her leg up under her skirt when the chain slithered from her flesh, scooting away from the male still looming over her, but she didn't make it far. Hand darting out to tangle in her tresses once again, he dragged her off the side of the bed.

Ezmira hit the floor with a painful thump. Twisting to get her feet under her put more tension on her scalp, causing her to let out a hiss.

He shifted his fingers. The pain lessened, but he didn't release his hold on her hair.

"I'll show you how this is for your protection."

Stomping to the door, the male pulled her along behind him. It was uncomfortable to walk hunched over with her head next to his hip, but he gave her no other choice.

It seemed to take an unusual amount of time for him to open the door, and after a moment, she realized the thumps and squeals were the locks being turned. She didn't know how many there were since she missed the first few, but she counted over five locks before the door opened.

Once through the doorway, he finally allowed her to stand upright, thrusting her out before him as he forced her down a short hallway. He must have grabbed a candle because the flickering light followed her, doing nothing to illuminate her path. The hall was in no better repair than the room, cracks running from floor to ceiling and plaster missing in areas, revealing the bones of the building. With him holding her hair, she couldn't watch her feet and tripped over something on the floor more than once, earning her an angry grumble and fresh burning in her scalp.

"This place is not safe. Only certain areas can still bear weight, and one wrong step will send you falling through the floors below."

The words were angry, his irritation evident, and it only flamed the fire burning in her veins higher.

"It's your fault I'm in this dangerous building! Why would you bring me here?"

His only response was a growl.

Shoved through the opening at the end of the hall, Ezmira found herself in a larger room with more murals on the ceiling and walls. With the number of missing pieces and amount of grime built up, it was impossible to tell what the image had been, but the space looked like some sort of museum.

"This is the safest place in Cryptik," he muttered as he continued pushing her forward.

The candle did little to light the room, but it was enough for her to see that one wall was a solid bank of windows with a pair of doors in the center. Many of the windows were missing or boarded over, leaving the room even chillier than his bedroom had been, and he seemed to be forcing her straight toward the doors.

Unsure what was beyond them, Ezmira dug her feet into the floor, trying to stop their forward motion, to no avail. The room had more litter than the hallway, causing her to trip every other step, and she finally had to give in or risk turning an ankle.

The alpha stopped before she hit the doors, reaching around her to pull the lock and open it before his humongous hand thrust her forward again. Her scalp had grown numb from his tight hold, but the wind that hit her as she stepped through brought a fresh wave of needling pain to the rest of her. Wrapping her arms around her body, it was hard to keep her teeth from chattering as he yanked her to the edge of the balcony.

"Look!"

Ruthless fingers forced her head forward, her hands instinctively reaching out to clutch the banister as a dizzying wave of nausea roiled in her stomach at the sight of how high they were. She hadn't known, and just the thought of potentially falling so far only to smack against the ground had her using all her meager strength to push herself back, but the wall of his body trapped her. Ezmira's one fear was heights, and just being close enough to see the ground had her knees going weak as fresh tears spilled.

A broad arm wrapped around her ribs, hoisting her up even as the other kept her facing that terrifying view. With her previous fears forgotten in the rush of a greater one, she clung to his arm and begged.

"Please! Please, no. Back inside! I'm sorry!"

Her voice came out on a strangled cry, the words broken and trembling in the wind.

"There are no stairs to get up here. No convenient ladders. This is the safest place because no one else can get up here, but if you don't know the handholds, you'd never make it down. Or at least not without a sudden, painful stop at the end. I didn't bring you here to die, you foolish woman, and you need me to keep you alive."

She nodded her head as much as his hold allowed.

"Yes. Yes, I understand. Please take me back in."

As scary as it was to be inside with him, the balcony was more so. The wind was so strong she worried it would push them over. She didn't know if it was her imagination or the sorry state of the building, but she swore she could feel them swaying in the wind.

The alpha grunted, putting her on her feet and finally releasing his hold on her hair. Grabbing her by the wrist instead, he turned back to the doors. Ezmira gladly followed him back in. When he stopped to close and lock the door behind them, she pressed her back to the wall, sucking in great gasps of air to calm her racing heart. Her fingers dug into the crumbling plaster at her back, reassuring her it was solid and she no longer hung in the open air.

The candle had blown out in the gust of wind from outside, but the alpha at her side relit it, the warm glow spilling over the dirty floor before he lifted it to shed light through the room.

"This is where you will dance for me. When you're not here, you'll be in the bedroom. The other rooms are not stable."

She nodded her head in acknowledgment, but didn't meet his gaze. Eyeing the state of the room, her expression grew critical. He must have noticed, because he snapped his question through gritted teeth.

"What?"

The word held enough growl to make her skin crawl, but despite her worry about angering him further, she couldn't hold back her own concern.

"I can't dance in here."

She peeked at him from the corner of her eye, watching his face darken as his free hand fisted at his side.

"You *will* dance for me."

Ezmira flinched away from the menacing snarl, fighting the urge to fall to her knees as dust trickled down from the ceiling.

"I can't! The floor... There's no space. I'll break an ankle if I try to dance in this mess."

She kept her head lowered, waiting for another terrifying outburst. His fury simmered in the silence. Her heart hammered in fear. She fought against the urge to shrink into herself when the crunch of plaster underfoot announced he was moving toward her.

His yank on her arm pulled her forward. She couldn't stop herself from looking up. The grip on her wrist was painfully tight, but he was walking slower than he had on the trip out to the balcony. With the light in front of her, she could pick her way over the worst of the debris, which held her attention until he led her back into his bedroom.

Placing the candle back on the mantel, he pulled her toward the bed. Heart lurching into her throat, she let her arm extend to the fullest when he turned to face her.

"Get on the bed."

His command was quiet, but it held no less strength for it. Debating the wisdom of fighting him versus doing as she was told, she decided the threat of falling to her death was worse than anything he could do to her, and she wasn't brave enough to find an alternate way down.

Swallowing her fear, she cautiously climbed onto the mattress, careful to keep her dress tucked around her. She frowned at how dirty the ends of her skirt looked, but she forced the trivial thought away. She remained silent and pliant as he changed his hold to her ankle, wrapping the chain around it once again. Though she winced with the click of the lock, she didn't see what other choice she had.

Not sure what was going to happen next, she watched the alpha as he moved around the bed. He stopped to stare down at the fireplace before looking back up at her, but instead of lighting it, he walked past to the door.

"Please! I'm so cold."

The wind outside had stolen what little warmth she'd had, and with the anger that had sustained her draining away, Ezmira shivered on the bed.

"I can't trust you not to burn down our only safety. There are two blankets on the bed. You'll be fine."

With that, he turned and walked through the door, closing it behind him. Her hands balled into fists, digging into the thin blankets beneath her as she scoffed.

"These hardly qualify as blankets," she muttered to herself before heaving a sigh. It wasn't like she had any other options, and he possibly had a point with his assessment. She might do something dumb if she thought it would earn her freedom, though the thought of being trapped in a fire so high off the ground sent a surge of bile up her throat.

Pulling the blankets tight around her, she rolled into a little ball on the side of the bed, fighting back the surge of tears that threatened to drown her again. Tears wouldn't help. They were in the early hours of the morning, and if she was going to be forced to dance for him while trying to plan an escape, she needed to get some rest.

Chapter 6

Quasim

Fatigue pulled at him, but Quasim refused to stop moving.

He always hurt worse when he stopped, and since he'd had such an active last few hours, he knew he'd suffer immensely the moment he quit pushing himself.

The contents of the bucket clattered as he tipped it over the side of the building yet again. He watched as the debris slammed to the ground below, adding to the piles already littered there.

As he turned to walk across the balcony, back into the massive room, a shadow shifted across the already darkened window in the building across the street. Freezing in place, he waited to see if it would shift again.

He'd thought he'd seen movement earlier too, but sometimes he couldn't trust his weakened eyes. Yet his instincts warned him of danger, so he remained still another moment and glared at the window.

If anyone was there, they might have heard his prize's high, feminine screams from earlier in the night. Might have seen the treasure he had hidden in his den.

Ice flooded his veins.

As though to prove his point of how cutthroat Cryptik could be, the wind carried sounds of fighting moments before the balcony trembled under his talons. He gripped the bucket and fought down nausea as the sound of a small pop followed the shudder. A corner of a smaller building down the street crumbled to the ground, several blocks away, but too close for comfort.

Quasim forced his legs to move, his terror battling with the misery of his wounds as he hobbled back to the gigantic room.

He couldn't let the precious omega hurt herself while under his care.

He laid the bucket on its side and swept the last bit of the pile of debris into it.

The scrape of glass shards and rock colliding as he forced them into the bucket brought back the memory of her screams.

He shouldn't have picked her up near the railing, but he needed her to fully understand the danger.

Quasim lifted the bucket and inspected the weighted ball of emotions in his gut.

Why did her screams bother him? He'd heard worse before, the sizzling of flesh and his own agonized bellows echoing in his mind.

She'd been frightened before he'd picked her up, but he hadn't believed her. When her slim fingers had clamped on his arms and she'd begged to move away from the ledge, his focus had been on making sure she wouldn't try to escape.

He understood now. She wasn't just scared of falling. A woman didn't scream like that only because she didn't like her situation. No, his prize was terrified of heights.

He should feel guilty for bringing her here, but he didn't.

The horizon lightened, signaling the rise of the sun as he stepped back onto the balcony. He dumped the bucket over the furthest corner and turned back to his sanctuary.

With crumbling spires and gargoyles disfigured by decay, the old building blended into the city's ambiance and matched the way his body felt. It stood taller than most, which gave him the advantage of looking down on any adversaries and knowing if trouble was coming. In the few years he'd lived there, no one had bothered him, even when he went to the market, but the omega's scent wafting up from his tattered pants changed everything.

He tossed the bucket into the corner before picking up the broom he'd bought when he'd first moved into the building. The bedchamber hadn't been easy to fix, but despite the paint chipping off the walls and dust lingering in the upper half of the room, it was more than sufficient for him.

He'd reinforced the floor beams and added locks to the sturdy door. His brothers would call his hideaway a bunker. A place of safety in a war zone.

This massive room off the balcony wasn't nearly as safe, but it was large enough for her to dance. He pushed the broom the length of the floor, lifting every speck of dirt and revealing smooth marble. As streaks of light peeked over the horizon, he finished sweeping and surveyed the room.

The floor didn't gleam, since it hadn't seen a polish in decades, but it would suffice. He dragged the only wooden bench that had been worth keeping to the wall near the hallway.

After staring at the only thing he hadn't touched yet, he limped to the covered item in the far corner of the room. Dust billowed into his face when he flung the ratty blanket off. The old music player looked to be in pristine shape, despite the chunks of wood missing from the bottom where the sheet hadn't quite covered it. Some of the falling plaster must have bounced after hitting the floor and banged into the base.

He shifted the amplifier, angling it toward the wall before lifting the lid and checking the inside. The spool of tines in the middle was perfect, as were the various cords and such running along the inside. He shut the lid and pivoted the horn back toward the center of the room. Two winds of the lever proved arduous but successful.

When he let go, the lever didn't move. Scowling, he ran his calloused hands along the outside until he found the switch tucked against the wall. Quasim flicked it upward and stepped back, almost snarling at the hideous grinding sound, but it evened out and began playing.

After a few warbled notes, it smoothed into a tune he hadn't heard in forever. It didn't match the style of songs she'd danced to the previous night, but he doubted there was any music she couldn't enchant him with.

He let it run for the last few moments he inspected the floor. With the morning sun brightening the sky, the light streamed in from the windows and lifted the gloom.

As he turned, his back spasmed so hard he grabbed for the wall to keep from falling. Tiny flakes of plaster drifted down to the marble when Quasim let go, but he couldn't wait any longer.

He needed the relief she could give him.

After torturing himself by forcing his spine as straight as he could manage, he picked up the broom and swept the flakes of plaster under the music box. He threw the broom into the corner with the bucket, angry at himself for needing any kind of help, and slammed the lever into its storage compartment. When the tiny door clattered closed, he flicked the hook into the little eyelet and turned away.

The damn thing had better work, or he'd chuck it off the balcony and watch it shatter on the street below. He'd make her dance in silence if necessary, but the thought only angered him more.

It was pathetic to need something so badly, but he couldn't change this. He growled and hunched, the strain on his mangled body too much to maintain an upright posture.

Furious by his predicament and yet excited to fall under his omega's spell, he turned to the hall and limped toward his bedchamber. He stopped halfway there, remembering the way she'd been shivering when he left.

She was so fragile, and he hadn't checked on her while he focused on his mission to clean the soon-to-be dance hall.

Despair rose in him as he realized he'd have to wait longer to watch her dance. She'd need things. Basic living requirements, like to relieve her bladder and take in sustenance.

He pushed down his dismay and mapped out the quickest way to provide for her morning needs.

Quasim ran down the checklist of foods he had and realized he'd have to make a trip to the market soon. He hadn't prepared to provide for another person, much less one as special as his prize.

He wasn't looking forward to visiting the busy market streets, but he would do whatever it took to take care of her so she could perform for him. That night, after he found relief from the terrible agony streaking the length of his spine, he'd make the daring trek to the city center for supplies.

Chapter 7

Ezmira

Ezmira jumped awake at the sound of the door crashing against the wall. Struggling out of the blankets that had done little to keep her warm, she peered up at the alpha standing in the doorway. His expression seemed to be a perpetual scowl, but after seeing the marks on his body, she knew he likely had reason for the foul visage.

She did her best not to shrink away as he stalked closer, but it was more than just instinct urging her to appear small and meek. After having a taste of his temper the night before, she wasn't ready for more.

His hand dug under the blanket, following the chain to her ankle and yanking it out. Despite still being dressed in only his ragged pants and no shirt, his palm burned against her skin; her hiss of discomfort causing him to look up at her as his hands worked the lock. She swallowed back the reaction, breathing a small sigh of relief as the metal left her leg.

"Up."

The alpha didn't give her time to follow the order before he took her by the arm and pulled her from the bed. Her indignant squawk didn't seem to faze him as he tugged her over to a curtain covering a portion of the wall, pulling it back to reveal a small bathing chamber.

"You have five minutes."

He propelled her into the room, releasing her arm and yanking the curtain shut in the same motion.

Ezmira looked around, hope daring to bloom in her chest as she thought she may finally escape, but it died just as quickly. There was no window large enough for her to slip through, even if the thought of falling didn't petrify her. The only opening was a narrow affair over the tub. Even her slim body wouldn't fit through.

In a nook with side columns and ornate carvings, the old-fashioned bath looked more like a massive cooking cauldron, and the towel hanging on the side was too small to climb down. There was no mirror or anything else she could fashion into a weapon, only a small area in the back with clothing hanging inside.

Unlike the other rooms she'd seen within the building, this one was spotless. Not a speck of grime marred the porcelain sink, though nothing would mend the chipped spots along the edges. No chunks of debris littered the floor, and no dust floated through the air. She supposed it made sense considering the alpha's injuries and the likelihood that the raw-looking flesh around his stumps could be prone to infection. In a way, it was a relief to see he was fastidious in this intimate, necessary space.

She had just finished her business and was washing her hands when the curtain jerked open once again. The big alpha glared at her as she dried off, then took her by the arm again.

"I can walk. You don't have to drag me around everywhere."

Her words had little effect, only earning her a grunt before he pushed her backward onto the bed.

"Sit. Eat."

He thrust a bowl at her chest, the grey mush inside making her lip curl. She tried to hold up her hands to push it away, but he only shoved the bowl into them, letting go before she could protest.

"Eat," he repeated, the stern command giving her no choice but to make the attempt.

Sitting gingerly on the edge of the mattress, she held the bowl with one hand while the other lifted the spoon. The smell wafting to her as it got closer to her face made her turn away, dropping the utensil back into the dish.

"I don't think I'm hungry."

He met her soft complaint with a growl, her stomach clenching and threatening to empty itself of nothing but bile if necessary. Lifting the spoon again, she held her breath while parting her lips. Even without smelling the gruel, she gagged when it hit her tongue. If someone left thick oatmeal in a rusty pot overnight after adding enough salt to dehydrate a horse, it would still taste better than the lump in her mouth.

Once the spoon passed her lips, the alpha walked away, coming back before she had the chance to spit out the food. He yanked the spoon out of her hand and replaced it with a cup. Looming over her with an expression that made it clear he would not leave until she finished it all, she finally gave in and forced the gruel down, tipping the rim of the bowl to her lips and fighting back a gag with each swallow. Several times, she swapped which hand she drank from, taking a sip of water to help the disgusting mess slide down her throat. When the gruel was gone, she chugged the rest to rinse the taste away. Her tongue still felt dry, but he took the dishes from her tense hands and neither asked if she wanted nor offered to get her more.

He disappeared for a moment before returning empty-handed. Reaching for her again, his scowl deepened when she flinched away.

"It's time for you to dance," he growled.

"Please..." Her thought trailed off as she realized she didn't know his name. "What do I call you anyway?"

Her question seemed to make him pause. His scowl lifted to a confused look before he straightened and cleared his throat.

"I am Staff Sergeant Quasim Odo."

He winced, shoulders hunching as the scowl returned and his tone turned mocking.

"Or I was. Before. Now it's just Quasim. The broken hunchback beast."

A lump filled Ezmira's throat as tears pricked the back of her eyes. He said the last words quietly, like they weren't for her ears. There was so much pain beneath the front he put on, it left her chest aching. No one deserved to feel so worthless and alone after surviving whatever he'd gone through.

Where was his family? Was he here because they'd shunned him? Or was this his choice? He didn't seem the type to accept help or want pity, and she felt sure his isolation was his own doing.

"Okay, Quasim. I'm Ezmira. You don't have to drag me around. I'll follow you wherever you need me to go."

Her quiet tone seemed to soothe a bit of his discomfort, and a small spark grew in her chest. This man had been through so much, lost too much, for her to fully understand what he was suffering. If all he sought was for her to dance so he could forget his pain for a short time, then she'd do it. Maybe if he was in a better mood, she could talk to him about getting back to her troupe.

"And you'll dance."

The demand came out slightly questioning, as if he didn't quite believe she was agreeing, but she nodded to assure him.

"I will."

He studied her a moment longer before turning to the door. This time, since he no longer held down her head, she could see how many locks barred the sturdy chunk of wood. Between that and the difficulty of even getting to his den, she wondered how much of a threat there really was and how much was paranoia from his trauma. He had said nothing, but the scars, along with his introduction, gave her a good idea. It could have been an accident, but as a former soldier, they were most likely from something far worse.

Standing, she moved to his side as he turned the last of the locks. Though he shot a glance at her, he didn't reach out to pull her along as he had before. She trailed behind him through the hall, careful of where she placed her feet until they reached the larger room. It was fully lit, with the sun glinting through the remaining pieces of colored glass, the broken panes allowing streaks of blinding light to shine onto the murals. Her breath caught in her throat as she realized why he'd taken hours to return to the room.

The entire floor was clean.

The chunks she'd tripped over the night before, the grit she'd felt beneath her shoes… all of it was gone.

"Oh my! Did you do this for me?"

Her eyes tipped up to Quasim's, but he turned away from her, one hand rising to rub the back of his neck before he dropped it and glared at her.

"You can't dance if you hurt yourself. Not like I had a choice."

Despite his gruff words, Ezmira had to bite back a smile. She had a feeling Quasim wasn't the callous, cruel alpha he'd portrayed himself to be the night before. Yes, he'd kidnapped her and was keeping her against her will, but there was still a heart buried somewhere in there, despite the scars it bore.

Reaching out, she laid a hand on his forearm. The minute she touched him, he froze, eyes widening as he stared down at her fingers.

Ezmira's gaze tipped down, taking in the contrast of her dark skin against his turquoise feathers, the down still soft despite the odd angles at which some of them lay.

"Thank you."

His throat worked, eyes still locked on her hand. Worry flashed through her as he kept staring at where their flesh touched, her heart thumping in fear, but his unblinking gaze seemed more like shock than anger. Like he didn't expect anyone to reach out.

Swallowing her own rising feelings, she let her fingers slip from his arm and took a few steps forward. There was plenty of space now—the only thing missing was something to dance to.

"Do you have music?"

Her question snapped him back into focus, his head jerking as he blinked at her before turning to the wall opposite the windows. There was an odd box on the floor, but as he opened the side and pulled out the lever, she realized it was an old music player. It wasn't one that allowed the user to choose what track played, coming standard with a certain set of songs, but it was what people once used when learning the steps to a dance, and it would work perfectly for her performance.

He cranked the lever, winding the old machine until the handle wouldn't turn any further. If she remembered right, they would play for a few hours before running out of power, so she sucked in a deep breath and prepared herself. She didn't have the proper shoes, so the ones on her feet would have to work, but at least she still wore the dress she'd performed in. She didn't like the idea of doing anything other than her best, even for an audience of one.

Even if that one had taken her against her will, manhandled her, and refused to let her go.

So what if he'd also shown moments of raw pain and loneliness? So what if he'd revealed an uncertain, desperate man who would stay up all night to make sure this room was safe for her? So what if her heart cried for the horrors he must have endured?

This wasn't about the size or quality of her audience.

This was about what flowed through her veins and the joy she felt in performing.

Well, the joy she remembered feeling when she performed.

Letting her breath out as the first notes filled the air, Ezmira slipped under the spell of the music, feet moving in patterns as ingrained as her name.

Chapter 8

Quasim

His talons stayed planted on the cold marble, but his soul lifted and swirled amid the grime-covered murals. With every step, she took him higher, until his agony disappeared and nothing remained except her grace.

Quasim stood entranced, uncaring when his shoulder seized and his lower back tightened. The elation sweeping through him urged him to move closer, but he stood as still as a statue, afraid to break the beautiful spell she wove.

Heat pressed into his flesh as the sun sparkled through the large stained-glass window along the center portion of the wall to his left.

Ezmira swirled and extended an elegant hand toward him before reaching toward the ceiling and bending so far backward her green hair brushed the floor, her lithe silhouette holding him captive. She reached into his soul and stole a piece of the writhing void he tried to keep locked away from the world, filling it with her dazzling beauty.

With every flick of her fingers and measured step of her dainty feet, she extracted his misery and sent him soaring higher.

The scars on his face pulsed and tightened, the rays of sun baking him until his skin felt scorched, yet he watched with rapt attention.

He plummeted as the music died an ugly, scratchy death and she stopped. Quasim snarled and stepped toward Ezmira, his seething rage bursting as high as she'd made him fly. The petrified fear shining from her glittering green eyes stopped him.

Sweat dripped from her temple and ran a tempting path down her throat. Lust twisted his stomach as he watched the bead of moisture slide over her collarbone and disappear between her luscious breasts. Ezmira's chest heaved, her dark skin hiding any flush she may have had, but the trace of arousal wafting from her snapped him out of his trance. He knew it was only an instinctive response. No one could want *him*.

Growling, both angry that she'd stopped and furious with himself for wanting her, he shook his head and turned away. Nothing could come from any attraction he felt for her.

She was an omega. Her body would respond to an alpha's call, even if that alpha was decrepit and unworthy.

Quasim moved to the music player, hesitating when he thought he saw her lips part as though to say something, but he shuffled closer to the box until he could grab the lever.

"Quasim?"

He paused, holding in the vicious rumble his chest longed to release.

Without her magic whirling around him, he felt his wounds more acutely than usual. His joints creaked like rusty hinges and his scars seemed to split open, the activities of the past day demanding their payment.

When he didn't respond, her skirt swished along the floor as she stepped closer.

"Can I have some water?"

Quasim let his eyelids droop as he sucked in a breath.

"Do not move," he snarled over his shoulder as he limped down the hallway. He knew she was terrified enough of the balcony that she wouldn't go out there by choice, and he'd boarded the interior door shut since the upper levels of the staircase had eroded long ago.

He grabbed the nearest cup in the bedchamber, filled it with water, and hobbled back to her. She stood where he'd left her, wariness emanating from her expression as he thrust the cup into her hands. He impatiently tipped the bottom when she acted like she was going to stop. He knew she hadn't drunk the entire thing, and he needed more of her dancing, so he didn't let her stop until the cup was empty.

His lungs filled with her delicious scent as he stood beside her, the slight tang of sweat teasing him. He wanted to lick up the trail of the bead he'd watched earlier, but she'd never welcome his touch.

When he snatched the empty cup from her, she looked at him with a furrowed brow.

"What?"

He didn't mean to snarl at her, but he hurt too much to temper his voice.

"N-nothing?"

He squinted at her until her eyes flicked to his hand. Not the hand holding the empty bottle. No, she gave an unconscious glance at his other hand, the one that should be empty.

It wasn't.

He cursed and pulled his digits out of her silky green tresses. Why hadn't she pulled away when his grotesque fingers invaded her locks?

Their eyes met for the briefest of moments before he cursed again and spun away. His lack of balance nearly sent him stumbling to his knees, but he pushed through the agony of twisted ligaments and limped across the room.

It took him a second to regain enough composure to reach down and grab the lever. His head swam as he stooped and cranked the music box, an odd combination of adrenaline and weariness pulling at him.

Ever since he'd become a prisoner of war, Quasim hadn't slept well, but he'd learned early on that letting himself get too exhausted gave the nightmares enough leeway to consume him. He'd overdone it, as evidenced by the confusion swarming him and his lack of control around the tiny omega standing across the dance floor.

Once the lever refused to wind any further, he released it and turned to Ezmira. She stood there, staring back.

He growled.

Vibrant green irises grew as her pupils shrunk, but, still, she didn't move. His control snapped, and he bellowed his rage.

"Dance!"

She jerked backward as though he'd struck her, but before he lifted his talons from the floor to go to her, she straightened her shoulders and lifted her chin.

The music drifted through the room, but her dance scooped him up and cradled him in comfort. With a flurry of skirts, she carried him away from his woes and showed him a world where atrocities didn't exist.

Shadows grew under the windowpanes until Ezmira's darkened outline mirrored her on the marble, stretched by the sinking sun. It was mesmerizing, watching her shadow chase her through her moves.

The heat lessened on his face as he watched her without the glare of evening streaming through the glass until something alerted him. The graceful arch of her spine shook, yet still she twirled and reached for him, siphoning off his pain.

His brow furrowed as her foot landed out of tempo with the music.

Ezmira's cute little antlers dipped toward him as she raised her hands, palms outward, and pivoted on the ball of her foot, creating a whirlwind of color and an invisible circle in the surrounding air.

His chest squeezed as her opposite foot landed completely off the beat, lowering almost too late for her to catch her weight. She stumbled but pulled herself up as though nothing had happened.

His talons lifted from the floor as she made another spin. Sweat no longer ran down her bosom, and as the truth slammed into him, his self-hatred grew. How could he be so blind?

She ended the spin with a graceful yet unsteady leg.

Quasim begged his knee to take his weight as he rushed toward her, but it sent pounding agony up his thigh when he forced himself forward.

Ezmira lifted her arms, spreading them in a beautiful pose before testing her precarious balance with a sensual, arduous stretch. As her body shifted to find the next stance, her vibrant green eyes turned unfocused and her shoulders wavered.

He darted forward but was too late.

Ezmira crumpled and her shoulder smacked against the hard marble before he reached her. He flung his left hand out, barely sliding it under her head before it cracked against the unforgiving floor.

His roar vibrated the rafters and loosened several panes of glass from their unsteady perches, sending shards skittering across the marble.

He was such a selfish idiot.

Omegas required more care than he'd given her. They needed more water than alphas did, even in normal circumstances.

Her predicament was anything but normal.

Quasim hung his head.

The moon mocked him, casting its cool light on his failure.

He'd forced this beautiful, fragile woman to dance for him all day long. He hadn't let her rest, or fed her, or even given her adequate water.

Turning her onto her back, he laid his ugly hand against her sternum and made sure her heart still beat. Its cadence was even, if a little fast, but her breath gradually slowed until he no longer worried he'd caused long-term damage.

He traced her warm cheek and marveled at its midnight tone. It should have highlighted the flamboyant clothing she wore, but he saw it the other way around. Her bright dress made him eager to touch her rich flesh.

Snatching his hand away, he rubbed the back of his neck before cursing out loud. Quasim scooped her into his arms and cradled her to his chest, turning from the room.

Even though she hardly weighed anything, he struggled to limp to the bedchamber. Once through the door, he used his back to shut it, gasping as agony speared down his spine from his stumps.

Refusing to fail her again, he laid her on the bed before engaging every lock on the door. He returned to her side and ran his knuckles over her cheek.

Alarm shot through him at how cold her face had become. He tested her bicep and found that it, too, was chilled.

Quasim prayed she'd lift her long eyelashes and bless him with her green irises, but she didn't rouse when he wrapped the two blankets around her. Growling and cursing under his breath, he hobbled to the mantel and picked up the log he'd dropped earlier and placed it in the fireplace. Within seconds, he had a decent fire burning, his previous preparations and years of practice aiding him.

The bed was too far away. It would take too long to warm her up.

Staggering to the chest by the hallway door, he spun the dials until the correct numbers faced him, then popped the latch and smacked the lid into the wall. He rummaged through to the bottom of the chest and grabbed the rolled up carpet he'd spent hours cleaning. It wasn't big, but neither was she.

Quasim dropped it by the fireplace only to slide it a few feet away, knowing he would build the heat source until the flames would be too dangerous to be so close to. After carefully spreading it with his talons, he shuffled to the bathroom and rummaged through the clothing enclave.

In the very back, zipped into a military clothing bag, hung a dreadfully thick fur vest. He'd never understood how anyone could come up with something so hideous but had learned there were worlds too cold to go to without such a monstrosity.

It had never fit him right. The large flap meant for covering and warming his wings had always made the collar pull on him weirdly, but now that he didn't have wings and wasn't active duty, he had no use for it. Why he'd kept it, and brought it with him, must have been insanity.

Except he was glad for that insanity, for the moment at least, because it meant more comfort for the woman he'd inadvertently abused.

He tore it off the hanger and limped back to the bedchamber. After spreading it over the fresh carpet, Quasim put more wood on the fire before leaning over the bed.

Ezmira was still so clammy his heart squeezed within his ribcage. He gathered her wrapped body and shuffled back to the fur mat he'd prepared for her.

She didn't respond when he placed her on it, and he couldn't deny himself a stroke of her hair.

When he stood and stepped toward the corner chair, thick emotions twisted his stomach. He shook while looking down at her. With her hair splayed around her head and her lower legs peeking out of the blankets, her innocence punched him in the gut.

Whatever she had or hadn't experienced in her life before he kidnapped her, she didn't deserve the treatment he'd given her.

He told himself it was guilt that moved him to sit down beside her and gather her into his arms. When her derriere settled on his lap, he hesitated. It wouldn't do to tempt himself. He was only trying to help her recover.

He needed her to dance, but what did she need?

She needed so much more care than what he'd given her. He'd never treat her so poorly again if it meant he'd miss her poise and her expressive eyes. Despite her lying still in his arms, she pulled on his soul, revealing emotions he'd never expected to experience again.

Quasim turned her so she sat between his legs with her back against his chest. Even that was too intimate.

He carefully shuffled her onto the side she hadn't landed on and faced her toward the fire. A groan left him as he rearranged himself so his hip rested against her back.

After a while, his hand moved of its own accord. She stole pieces of him no one should have access to. She didn't deserve the pain and memories he'd thrust at her.

He told himself he wanted to give her the same comfort she gave him, but he knew it was a lie. His fingers stroked along her skin because he was selfish and weak.

Ezmira was perfection. He was a catastrophe.

He'd have to do better. She'd never have to suffer because of him again.

And if, after a while, he gathered her into his arms, it was so she was more comfortable, not because he couldn't bear the distance between them.

Chapter 9

Ezmira

Warmth surrounded her, a delicious scent tickling Ezmira's nose and making her let out an interested hum. Her mind was fuzzy with exhaustion and all she wanted to do was slip back into sleep, but her tired stretch awakened a throbbing pain in her feet and calves. Her brows pinched, a frown crossing her face as more awareness returned.

Why did she hurt so much?

Struggling to open her eyes, bright light blinded her further, and she realized she was right in front of the fireplace. She jerked away from the flames and slammed back against something hard. When she swung her gaze behind her, she froze.

A broad swath of marred turquoise skin was inches from her cheek, the scent surrounding her that of an alpha male. Letting her eyes travel upward, the look on Quasim's face caught her off guard. Pain still lingered in the corners of his eyes, but there was a softness… A look of awe that made her heart clench. It melted the fear that had filled her when she realized she was sitting in his lap.

It took a moment longer to notice her legs stuck out at the end of the blankets he'd wrapped her in, and his hand was moving up and down her bare skin.

"Are you… petting me?"

Quasim's chest vibrated, releasing a noise that had the tension in her body bleeding away, though worry still tickled at the edges of her mind. Sensations tingled along her flesh, a throbbing beginning where her thighs met.

"So soft."

The words were so quiet she almost didn't catch them. Despite the soft purr vibrating into her, the hairs on the back of her neck stood up and the relaxation of his purr disappeared. She shouldn't be letting this man hold her, much less touch her so intimately.

"Could you let me go?"

She tried to keep her voice calm, so as not to upset him, but his head jerked up at her question as if she'd slapped him. The open expression on his face disappeared behind the hard facade he usually kept in place before he abruptly sat her on the floor and backed away. He tried to mask it, but she sensed the hurt she'd caused in his moment of vulnerability.

Opening her mouth, she couldn't find anything to say before he turned his back on her. The sight of his mangled flesh caused her to wince and pull away, knowing why he thought she asked him to stop. She was trying to think of a way to apologize without hurting him more when he came over and sat a bowl in her lap.

The sight of the same grey mash, even more congealed than that morning, forced an unstoppable retching noise from her throat. Pinching her eyes closed, she turned her face toward the fire, trying to come to terms with choking down more of it. Her body needed food, but her stomach rebelled at eating more of the gruel.

"You need to eat."

Nodding at his gruff assertion, she gripped the spoon sticking out of the bowl but still couldn't force herself to open her eyes and lift it to her lips. Fighting back tears of frustration, she sucked in a deep breath and looked up at him.

"Thank you for the food. It's just… different."

His brows tipped down, but he didn't appear angry. Eyes moving from her face to the bowl, he shifted from one talon to the other before looking away.

"What do you usually eat?"

He turned and walked toward the trunk against the wall, his movements stiff. Knowing she was helping him forget his pain while she danced had kept her going, giving her a greater sense of fulfillment than she'd had in a long time, but it was obvious nothing she could do would truly help him.

"I love fresh fruit, and I'm a glutton for bread. I like most things really, I just…" She paused, searching for a polite way to phrase the issue with the gruel. It was completely unappetizing, but she couldn't say that. "I just rarely use that much seasoning."

She winced as the words left her, but it was the best she could come up with.

"There's no fresh anything available in Cryptik. The only thing I have is some jerky."

The thought of more salt-laden food had her mouth puckering, but it couldn't be any worse than what was in the bowl. Quasim didn't give her the chance to decide, taking the bowl from her lap and pressing a strip of meat into her palm.

Giving a cautious sniff when he turned away, her tongue darted out to taste the tip before taking a bite. It was surprisingly good, apparently dried without the use of salt as she'd expected.

Before she knew it, she'd devoured the entire piece and was licking her fingers clean. A glance up showed Quasim staring at her. She froze, her cheeks heating in embarrassment.

"That was good. Thank you."

There was a moment of silence before he nodded and dragged his eyes away from her. Looking down at her hands resting in her lap, she wondered what was next. She was still slightly hungry but didn't want to ask for more since she wasn't sure what Quasim's situation was. If the entire city was in the same state as the building they were in, food could be scarce.

"Get on the bed."

Her breath caught when he gave the order, the startled glance at his face a natural reaction. She believed he wouldn't intentionally hurt her, but he was still an alpha and she an omega. She'd be unwise to expect him to not want certain things, especially with her at his mercy.

Moving slowly, she did as he ordered, keeping the blankets clutched around her as she crawled over the foot of the bed and took her place with her leg extended to where the chain rested. His hands were gentle as he wrapped it around her ankle, and he took a moment to stroke his thumb along her calf before stepping back.

He reached for a cup on the mantel, passing it to her before looking around the room.

"I need to go out. Get some rest. Don't…" His expression tightened when he paused, scrunching into his usual angry glare before he finished. "Don't be stupid."

Chapter 10

Quasim

Even in the middle of the night, the market teemed with creatures haggling for wares. The few square blocks where merchants sold their goods were the only relatively safe place in Cryptik. It was the only area where the authorities dared to enforce the rules, since failing to do so would cause the neighboring cities to report them to the crown. This was why the gangs never infiltrated, because they wanted their corner of the world to stay just as it was—controlled by them, not some uppity king who would make them walk the straight and narrow.

Quasim held in his growl, knowing it wouldn't serve him well as he gestured to the fat loaf of bread in the center of the seller's glass box. The beta, a mix of reptilian races, looked at Quasim's clothes and scars, obviously skeptical when he pointed at the price he'd written on his sign.

When Quasim nodded, the man stuck his scaled hand out, palm up, but Quasim scowled at him and shifted his hand toward a smaller, denser loaf of bread in the corner.

"That too. And two pounds of dried meat."

Quasim usually hunted and dried his own meat, but he couldn't leave Ezmira long enough to do that, and he was too low to go without. The thin merchant looked behind Quasim and flicked his eyes over their surroundings, no doubt worried Quasim planned foul play.

Understanding the man's reticence, Quasim pushed aside his tattered cloak and reached into his pocket. He pulled out the full amount before giving the beta the most secure form of reassurance he could. After dropping his already laden pack a foot in front of the cart, he slid the money on the counter and shuffled backward a few steps.

The guy's scales changed from light grey to almost black as he relaxed. He slipped a key from his pocket and wrapped both loaves in individual papers before sticking them in a bag and setting them on the counter. As he stepped to the other end of his shop, he locked the glass box and stooped to the lowest shelf.

"Not that. The real stuff. Under there," Quasim rumbled, pointing to the locked chest hidden under the glass box.

The beta's long tongue flicked out and licked his eye in a nervous gesture. He straightened to his full height, counted the money on the counter, then retrieved the jerky Quasim had paid for. Many of the merchants sold anything they could get their hands on as "meat", but Quasim would only have the best for his prize.

Once he relocked and stowed the chest, the thin man pushed the purchases to the edge of the counter and met Quasim's stare.

Quasim limped forward, picked up his bag, and carefully situated the food into the top of it. When he turned to leave, the shop owner surprised him.

"Thank you, sir. I'll remember you next time. Also…"

"What?"

Quasim was too tired to deal with niceties, so he didn't even care when his voice came out scratchy and abrupt.

"I had a special shipment come in, if you have any cash left."

"Of what?"

"Apples."

Quasim's heart sped up. He'd seen fresh fruit at Armyn's coronation ball, but he couldn't stomach food with so many people around. He couldn't remember the last time he'd seen it before that.

Plus, Ezmira had said she loved fresh fruit. He wanted to watch her expression as she bit into a ripe, juicy apple that he'd given her.

"How much?"

They haggled over the price quickly, neither one wanting to linger over the subject. Once they came to an agreement, Quasim hid them in the middle of his pack, which meant he had to let a few pieces of fabric hang out of the top, but he tightened the closure so nothing would fall out.

He said a gruff thanks, then took a roundabout way back home, making sure no one followed him. After dragging his exhausted body up a few flights of stairs, he rolled his shoulder and ignored the pain lancing into his spine.

He was almost to safety.

Launching himself across the gigantic hole in the floor left him shaking and gasping, his muscles straining to keep him from falling. He clambered to the outside of the building and focused on each handhold. They seemed further apart than normal. His talons slipped, and for a frightful second, he thought he'd fly for the last time before meeting the unforgiving ground below, but his gnarled fingers caught the edge of the trellis and he regained his footing.

With his heart in his throat, he finished his climb and stumbled across the balcony. After locking the door behind him, he shuffled through the darkened dance studio, the memory of Ezmira's nimble dancing bolstering him.

He limped down the hallway and unlocked the bedchamber as quietly as possible.

The embers cast the room in a faint glow, showing Ezmira curled in a tiny ball in the very center of the bed. Her green hair shimmered around her, but the rest of her hid under the blankets.

Shame filled Quasim as he realized how threadbare his sheets were. He'd offered this beautiful omega the most pitiful nesting material.

His fatigue lifted away as he thought of his impulse buys.

Despite his stealth, the moment he shut the door behind him, Ezmira popped to a sitting position. With her eyes wide and her hair sticking every which way, she looked frazzled.

"I need the bathroom. Please, I drank so much water!"

Setting the bag next to the door, Quasim yanked his keys out of his pocket and grabbed her ankle. The second he unlocked her cuff, she scrambled off the bed and darted into the bathroom.

Watching the curtain swish closed behind her, he rubbed the back of his neck before dropping his hand to his side.

Would she try to run if he didn't chain her? She'd been so terrified when he'd taken her to the balcony, he doubted she'd try to climb down, if she ever found the path, and he'd boarded up the most dangerous areas of the building.

Could he trust her not to steal his only form of genuine relief? Leaving her chained had seemed like the safest option, but what if something had prevented him from returning? Or if there was a disaster in his absence?

She couldn't even go to the bathroom if he chained her to the bed.

Maybe... maybe he'd been wrong to restrain her, but he'd needed to protect her from herself.

He looked down to inspect the chain and cursed his wayward hand. The ridiculous thing had buried itself in the sheets and was still warm from her body.

Quasim snatched his hand back and stomped to the bag. His entire back seized when he picked it up, forcing him to brace his palm on the door until his muscles relaxed.

Swimming in agony, he engaged every lock on the door before hugging the pack to his chest and hobbling to the dresser he used for cooking.

He hadn't handled bread or fresh food in so long, he had to dig deep in his memory to remember how to care for it. After pushing the top items in the bag aside, he pulled out the apples and the bread, setting them on the dresser before diving back into the bag.

He squirted a few drops of tasteless sanitizer on his hands, rubbed it in, then dug to the bottom of his pack. The small squares of cheese and jerky joined the other things on the dresser before he dragged the bag to the wall beside the bathroom.

Quasim pulled a clean plate from the crooked top part of the dresser and cut a slice from each of the loaves. He placed them on the plate before cutting a piece of cheese and adding it.

His hand ached from gripping the knife, but he welcomed the pain.

She was worth it.

After finding a medium-sized chunk of jerky and dropping it onto the middle of the plate, he popped a few chunks into his mouth and ate them while he closed everything up. It wasn't as flavorful as the meat he cured himself, but it was fresher and would do for the time being.

The water turned on in the bathroom as Ezmira flushed and washed her hands.

When she didn't immediately come out, he called her name.

"Yes?"

She didn't sound right, so he pushed open the curtain and stepped inside.

Ezmira stood looking down into the sink with her hands gripping the edge. With her shoulders hunched, she looked up at him with startled eyes.

He took in her stance and snarled.

Before she could shrink away, he scooped her up, ignoring the agony coursing through his body.

He carried her to the bed and sat her on the edge, but when he went to stand, her tiny fingers gripped his bicep.

"I'm sorry. I'm fine."

Her words made no sense, so he shoved them away and inspected her from head to toe.

Quasim couldn't see anything wrong, so he brushed her hair out of her face and met her gorgeous green eyes.

Neither spoke. He couldn't figure out what to say, and her scrunched brows showed her confusion.

Quasim turned and lurched away, growling at himself. He snatched up an apple, washed it in the bathroom sink, then put it on her plate.

She sat exactly where he'd left her, looking uncertain. He shoved it on her lap and forced his talons to carry him to the chair in the corner. Once there, he couldn't bring himself to sit. His body hurt too much.

Her gasp lingered in the silence.

"All this is for me?"

How could someone so beautiful also have such a delicious voice?

Quasim grunted and motioned for her to eat.

"Thank you."

He would have shrugged, but his shoulder chose that moment to cramp and send him deeper into a hunch.

Ezmira's eyes widened and worry flickered across her features, but he turned away. He didn't need pity.

"Eat."

Quasim hated being so weak, so even though a part of him preened under her attention, no matter the reason for it, he brushed her concern away and hobbled to the fireplace. He angled his body so he could watch her eat while he built the fire back to its blazing glory.

Her first bite of bread nearly brought a moan to his lips. The joy on her face lit his heart with pride and sent tendrils of heat into his veins.

The second piece of bread filled her delicate fingers, her hunger evident in the speed with which she brought it to her mouth, and he stared in awe as she bit down.

Yearning filled him. The warmth sparking through him morphed into sharp shocks, like lightning coursing through his loins.

Quasim couldn't force himself to look away, even as the blood boiling like lava within his veins threatened to drown him. As the plate emptied, her movements slowed until each bite held a sensual note.

Without meaning to, she tempted him.

He wanted to taste her lips and enjoy the residual sweetness of the apple, knowing her flavor would be much more satisfying.

The second he realized the direction of his thoughts, he switched them off. Yet, despite the circumstances of her arrival and every horrible thing he'd done to her since she woke, the floral scent of her arousal hung faintly in the air.

Quasim yanked his control tight against his wounds, using his agony to propel himself away from the fire. He jerked the plate out of her lap and picked up the chain. When he pulled it toward her, she swung her leg onto the bed.

Quasim noted her grimace but locked the cuff around her ankle and forced himself away.

After washing the plate, he grabbed two cups, filled them with water, handed one to Ezmira and left the other on the floor next to the bed.

Not trusting himself to speak, he hobbled into the bathroom and made sure the curtain closed all the way before turning on the bath water.

He needed to soak and ease his overworked wounds before he could trust himself to interact with her again.

Shucking his pants off took more effort than he expected. His cock hated being denied, but the damn thing could suffer, just like him. It had picked the worst time to prove it still worked.

Ezmira deserved better.

Quasim's life held only one thing. Suffering. He'd have nothing more.

She'd dance for him, and that was it. The situation he was in was his own punishment for kidnapping a female, and he deserved the pain.

Quasim hissed as he lowered his ruined body into the hot water. Once he loosened his muscles and lost his hard-on, he'd make sure Ezmira needed nothing else.

Propping the base of his skull on the edge of the basin, Quasim stared at the ceiling and thought about her sitting on the bed. Her skirts were dirty. She'd grimaced in pain.

He decided she'd bathe once he finished, since the water would still be warm but not as hot as he needed it. That way, they wouldn't waste water or overwork the water heater.

With the next step plotted in his mind, he tried to relax in the water so the heat could do its job.

Chapter 11

Ezmira

Her mind whirled, not sure what to make of the conflicting feelings clogging her chest.

Quasim had kidnapped her. He held her captive, gave her the bare minimum of necessities, and demanded more from her than she'd ever given in a dance.

And yet he seemed to regret his actions even as he performed them. He was gentle with her when he remembered to be, and he'd gotten her better food. She did not know what his economic state was, but from what she could see, he didn't appear to have much, and guilt gnawed at her belly thinking he'd given so much just to get her the things she liked.

Sighing, Ezmira rolled over. There was a splash from the bathroom, reminding her of the sweat built up on her skin. Her flesh prickled with the sensation of something crawling on her, causing her to shudder. She'd love the chance to bathe, but she wasn't sure how Quasim would react if she asked.

She startled upright when he threw the curtain open, his swirling grey eyes meeting hers. The signs of pain around his eyes had lessened, and with the shift in countenance, his handsomeness struck her despite the scars. She'd first recognized his good looks in the few moments she'd looked at him while she danced, when the scowl was absent and he seemed at peace.

He was wearing another torn pair of pants like his previous ones, leaving his chest bare. Water still matted the feathery down covering his abs, a droplet slipping free to trail down to where the pants hung low on his hips.

Ezmira couldn't force her eyes away, mouth going dry at the obvious bulge beneath the fabric. Surly at best, her captor was still an alpha, and his body called to her base nature. It was impossible not to take notice.

Swallowing hard, she snapped from her trance when he moved to the side of the bed and reached for her foot. Her heart still quickened each time his fingers skimmed her flesh, but instead of shivering away from the touch, she wanted to press herself into it.

What was she thinking?

The clank of the chain brought her mind back into focus as Quasim stepped back and gestured to the bathing chamber.

"There's water. Should still be warm. Go wash."

It was reflex to smile in excitement, though she realized the reaction may seem strange. Being allowed to bathe shouldn't be something she got excited about, but it was exactly what she'd wanted, and she'd take what she could get.

Scrambling off the bed, she made her way around him and slipped into the little alcove, pulling the curtain closed behind her. She stared at it for a moment, wondering if it was smart to trust him not to come through the flimsy door when she had no clothes on, but he'd had ample opportunity to take advantage of her if he'd wanted to.

Peeling off her dress, she felt a brief pang at how dirty it was. After two grueling dances and wearing it for so long, the once beautiful performing gown had distinctly wilted, and she wasn't sure she could ever return it to its former glory.

Sighing, she dropped it and pushed the thought aside. Material things shouldn't matter when she didn't know what was going to happen to her. She could continue searching for an escape, but it was getting harder to imagine a successful one. If what Quasim told her was true, he could leave all the doors open and she'd still be in the most effective prison he could have found.

Then there was the growing feeling of connection between them. The way he looked at her like she was all he needed in the entire world. It was hard not to crave that feeling when she'd struggled to find herself for so long.

Reaching out, she dipped a hand into the water, Quasim's scent rising to tease her nostrils. She felt her nipples pebble in response to the smell of his arousal, her body reacting to his as nature intended. She'd never felt such an attraction to an alpha's scent outside of heat, and she couldn't help marveling at the sensation while she had a clear head to explore it.

Was it only because he was an alpha, or was there more to this pull between them? Their circumstances should have her terrified of him, not giving her all to help him as much as she was able, but underneath the selfish appearance of his actions, she could sense the desperate longing for peace. Many people made questionable choices under the influence of pain, and he'd respected her boundaries when she asked him to stop.

Groaning under her breath, Ezmira rubbed her face before gripping the side of the tub and stepping in. The water was slightly cooler than she preferred, but she was grateful there was running water in the building at all. Having heated water was a luxury.

She didn't waste time as she cleaned herself, using the bar of soap she found on the windowsill. It smelled even more strongly of Quasim, making her traitorous belly clench at the thought of rubbing his scent all over her.

Ezmira wasn't sure what to do with the water when she finished, so she decided asking was the best option. Stepping out of the tub, the only thing she could find to dry with was a tiny towel hanging over the sink. She wrung her hair out as much as she could, but she'd soaked the towel before she'd gotten her hair anything less than dripping. The dampness in the cold was a recipe for illness, but she had little choice.

Unwilling to pull on her dirty dress again, she wrapped the towel around body, the edges barely meeting and the fabric ending at the top of her thighs. Sucking in a deep breath to steady her nerves, she pulled back the edge of the curtain and poked her head out, finding Quasim standing in front of the fireplace.

"Do-Do you have a shirt I could borrow? Or something? My dress is pretty dirty."

He turned to face her, frowning as he took in the way she hid behind the curtain, but he moved to a pack resting against the wall. His slow movements as he leaned down to reach into it showed that the bath hadn't helped his pain for long, but he distracted her from thinking about that when he straightened with a handful of colorful cloth.

"I saw these when I went out."

He thrust them at her as if the fabric might hurt him. The feel of the silky cloth as she took it caused her to gasp, her eyes widening at the softness. The clothes were a little worn, the hems frayed in places, but as she shook out the shirt, she decided they were still beautiful.

"Th-Thank you!"

Ezmira backed into the bathroom again, putting her back to the opening so she could hold up the clothing and get a better look. The top was a bright pink, with pretty teal shapes along the bottom edge. It was long, with the hem coming down to a point in four places before curving up to dip to the next point. Most people would think the purple tights were too much for the brightness of the top, but Ezmira loved it, thinking they paired perfectly.

Dropping the towel, she pulled the shirt over her head before shimmying into the tights. They ended just below her knee, and she had no underthings to wear beneath them, but she was happy to have something clean.

Turning to head back to the other room, her heart stumbled at the sight of the partially open curtain. She hadn't thought to pull it closed in her haste to get into the new clothing. Though she couldn't see Quasim, she knew he'd been just on the other side after handing her the fabric, and the thought of him seeing her naked brought a rush of heat flooding through her body to pool in her belly.

Swallowing the reaction, she could only hope he'd turned away before she'd dropped the towel. A quick peek through the opening showed Quasim on the other side of the room, so she sucked in a deep breath and emerged.

"Thanks again. They're lovely," she murmured as she stopped by the bed. She bowed her head, fingers playing with her tunic's hem when he turned to face her.

She didn't know what time it was in the dark room, but it felt like the middle of the night, and the events of the past two days were catching up with her. Energy suddenly draining from her body, she sagged with exhaustion. While the soreness had left her calves, her feet were still achy, and she wanted nothing more than to curl up on the bed and go to sleep.

"You're welcome."

Not sure what else to do, Ezmira climbed onto the mattress, extending her leg toward the chain and looking up at Quasim. His expression seemed torn, and he hesitated before shaking his head.

"Just go to sleep. It won't be long till morning."

Breath catching in her throat, she pulled her leg closer to her body, giving him a smile as she wrapped her arms around her knees. It had been hard to get comfortable with the chain on, and the metal chaffed her skin.

"Thank you," she murmured again.

It was hard to fight the urge to cry. She wasn't even sure why she felt the need, only that every interaction with Quasim left her more confused. He'd inadvertently convinced her he was a good man beneath his pain and heartache.

All she received in response was a grunt as he moved in front of the fireplace again. As she laid down and pulled the blankets over her, she felt another settle on top, drawing her attention back to the big male.

Eyes glancing down at the quilt, she smoothed her hand over it before looking back up at him and smiling again. She had to strangle the urge to giggle as the thought entered her mind that he was really a big softy underneath the gruff exterior. Trauma may have scarred his heart to match his flesh, but he still wanted to be good.

Closing her eyes, she'd almost drifted off when she felt the mattress dip as a heavy weight settled onto the other side of the bed.

Bolting upright, her wide eyes turned to take in the sight of Quasim stretched out on his side next to her. She slipped off the edge of the bed before she had time to think, standing and staring down at him.

"What are you doing?"

The question burst from her in the same way her heart threatened to burst from her chest. Had she only fooled herself into thinking she was safe with him?

His brow lowered as he opened his eyes to glare at her.

"This is my bed. I'm going to sleep."

Her mouth opened and closed, her mind stumbling over what to say. He had done nothing indecent to her yet, but that didn't mean she trusted him enough to want him in bed with her.

"Either lie down here or sleep on the floor. I don't care what you do."

His face turned away from her, eyes closing as if he couldn't care less. His actions left her gaping, her earlier warm feelings having fled.

Eyeing the small space left on the bed, she turned to look at the rug in front of the hearth. The floor was hard, but at least it offered some cushion.

Moving to kneel on it, she looked up at the bed again. Quasim didn't move, the slow rise and fall of his shoulder making him appear to be already asleep.

Chapter 12

Quasim

He was making another faux pas, he knew, but Quasim hurt too much to even entertain the idea of sleeping on the floor.

Despite understanding why she'd reacted the way she had, her sudden change from soft and smiley to scared and appalled rankled him more than he cared to admit. Quasim knew he should be used to it by now, but he'd spent as much time avoiding others as they had him, so he did not have as much practice as he could have. Plus, she'd tugged on his heart in a way he doubted he'd ever be prepared to deal with.

She knelt next to the fire, looking between the fur he'd placed there and where he lay, no doubt wondering if even that much space was enough to stay safe from him. She was smart to be wary of alphas, since their intentions regarding an omega were rarely innocent.

The firelight danced across her delicate features, highlighting her full lips and wide eyes, and with the bright pink shirt she wore, her green hair seemed to shimmer more than before. Her matching green irises flicked to the floor again before she lowered herself and balled up under her blankets.

He needed sleep like a dehydrated omega needed water, yet he couldn't take his eyes off her beautiful face until it wavered and he could no longer hold his eyelids open.

Like always, he fought sinking too deeply into dreamland, knowing the horrors waiting for him there. Visiting his memories always resulted in terrible nightmares.

If he had napped during the day, as had become his habit, then he would close his eyes with a bit more confidence, but he hadn't slept for two days.

As his eyelids drooped even though he fought to hold them open, dread built in his chest. It had been longer than two days since he'd laid down, much less slept. The coronation had rocketed his stress levels so high he hadn't rested well for several days before either.

When he lost sight of Ezmira's form and couldn't lift his lids for another peek, he knew he'd failed her yet again. His demons were already reaching for him, pulling him under to torture him once again.

At least she had been smart and chosen to lie next to the fire, far away from him.

Darkness stole the present and shoved him into hell on earth. No matter how hard he tried, there was no escape.

His enemies held him.

They had no mercy.

Chapter 13

Ezmira

The rug did nothing to soften the floor. Even with how sore and tired her body was, it still rebelled against falling asleep in front of the hearth. The heat that felt so good from a distance was too much up close, and Ezmira had to bite back the whine that wanted to escape.

Sitting up, she pushed the hair out of her face, glaring at the lump on the bed that still hadn't moved. She didn't know how long she'd tossed and turned on the floor, but Quasim slept, unaffected by her discomfort.

She grumbled under her breath. It was her own fault since she'd chosen the floor over lying beside him. He may have kidnapped her, but the sight of his stumps reminded her she couldn't put him out of his own bed. It would be cruel to demand he give up the comfort for her.

Rolling onto her knees, she stared at the slumbering alpha. He clearly had no intentions for her, or he would have taken one of the many opportunities he'd already had. It wasn't like she hadn't shared a bed with a few select troupe mates when they couldn't afford extra rooms. But none of them were strangers.

Or alphas.

Shaking off the crawling sensation in her limbs, Ezmira pushed to her feet, eyes never leaving Quasim. She slinked closer, hesitating before gingerly placing her weight on the edge of the bed. He didn't move or give any sign that he was aware of her presence, so she forced herself to relax and pull the blanket over her, careful not to bump the sleeping male. They were both dressed and there were blankets separating them. The worst that could happen would be that he rolled over and squashed her or she moved and hurt one of his stumps.

It was a few minutes before she could let her eyes drift closed, and even more before the tension left her body, but she was too tired to keep her vigil for long. Slipping into sleep, she couldn't help but think what it would be like to share a bed with him every night, with his enormous arms locked around her as he purred his contentment in her ear.

She had no clue how long she slept, only that it wasn't long enough. The fire had burned down and there was a heaviness in the air that made her think it was the early hours before dawn. She didn't know what had woken her since her body still begged for more rest.

Sighing, she relaxed back onto the pillow until the mattress jolted again. A low growl filled the room, slamming her heart into her throat as images of the building collapsing with them in it filled her head.

Sitting up, Ezmira turned to look at Quasim to see what was wrong, but he had his eyes pinched closed. His head tossed from side to side, mumbled words pouring from his lips as he grimaced in pain.

"Quasim?"

She spoke as softly as she could with her heart threatening to burst from her chest, but he still jerked, legs thrashing. She felt one of his talons catch the flesh of her leg, but the sting was a distant pain as she focused on the man beside her. His eyes remained shut as if he were trying to run from something in his dreams, and she wasn't sure if she should wake him or not.

"Quasim?"

She added a little more force to her voice. He stilled for a moment before a pain-filled cry rent from his throat. Reaching out to lay a hand on his shoulder, she hesitated before letting their flesh connect. She knew waking someone from a nightmare could be risky, but she couldn't listen to him suffering a moment longer.

Pressing her palm to his upper arm, she gave a gentle shake as she called his name again.

"Quasi-ahh!"

The word ended in a startled scream as his thick digits wrapped around her throat and shocked the sound to silence before his dark eyes flashed open. Her back slammed into the mattress, head bouncing on the pillow as Quasim straddled her hips. His snarls filled the room as his blank gaze locked on her face, but he didn't see her. His mind wasn't in the room with her.

She struggled under his weight, both hands clutching the wrist attached to the hand strangling her. Her pulse pounded in her face as he tightened his grip and cut off her circulation. Her bucking did nothing to dislodge the massive male.

Scratching at his forearms as her lungs screamed for air, tears leaked from the corners of her eyes. She knew something horrible had happened to Quasim and, whatever it was, it held him trapped in its embrace.

As he leaned down over her, she regretted what she needed to do, even as she reached under his arm and dug her fingers into the scars on his back. His cry of misery matched the pain in her heart.

Chapter 14

Quasim

As fresh as the day they held glowing-hot iron against his stumps to stop him from bleeding to death, overwhelming agony speared into his spine and launched into his brain.

His gnarled hand lost their enemy's throat and shot to his skull, providing counter pressure to the pain even though he knew the damage was already done and nothing would ease his misery. Curling in search of relief, a warm, thin arm got stuck between his bare chest and his bicep, and the second he realized who it was, Quasim straightened and flung himself off the bed.

In his millisecond of airtime, his self-hatred skyrocketed. She'd been so desperate to get him off her she'd grabbed his stump, and when he'd curled inward, he'd trapped her arm to him.

He couldn't breathe through the impact with the floor, and for several seconds, Quasim could only lie on his side and silently roar at himself. When his diaphragm relaxed and he pulled oxygen into his lungs, he rolled to his stomach and fought his way to his knees.

He hadn't hurt so much or been this stiff since waking up for the first time at the hospital. Taking the omega was supposed to help him, but he was only causing himself more misery. He was inflicting his woes on someone else, someone who didn't deserve to carry his burden.

Ezmira finally made a sound as he clamped a hand on the edge of the bed and pulled himself up so he could see her. The band of worry cranked tighter around his chest, stopping his ability to speak.

He had a new nightmare to look forward to: the memory of dark, silky skin encompassed by hate-filled gnarled hands as gorgeous green eyes glazed with death.

It got worse when the scent of her blood filled his nostrils.

His broken half moan, half growl filled the silence.

When his eyes finally focused on the present, she'd gained enough breath to steal his own.

Tears dripped down her temples as she lay flat on her back, still sunken deep into the mattress. He searched for the source of her bleeding, terrified he may have done irreparable damage. Starting from the top of her head, he skimmed downward, noting the marks on her neck where his hand had been, until he found the scratch along the inside of her left calf. It didn't look deep, but fresh crimson trailed down onto the sheets. Thick grief, fear, and anger clogged his throat as he looked back toward her face. Her eyes turned to his and shattered what little remained of his heart.

Quasim couldn't open his mouth. His jumbled emotions stole his voice. She spoke first and broke the tether to his restraint.

"I'm s-sorry!"

Her scratchy apology made no sense. Rage burst from him, but not toward her. He'd never hated himself more.

"Don't apologize! Who the hell apologizes after someone attacks them? No, don't move, Ezmira."

She stopped trying to sit up and sank back into the bed.

"I almost fucking *killed* you!"

She flinched at his roar but stayed where she was, her body shaking as sobs built in her chest.

His anger broke and left him with the horror of what he'd just done.

Quasim did the only thing he could.

He purred.

Even knowing she should despise him, he extended a shaking finger and ran it across her cheekbone, urging her to relax.

Ezmira cried as his purr melted the tension from her muscles. Quasim lost himself in her sweetness, lightly tracing the trail of her tears before ghosting his fingers over the bruising flesh of her throat.

His soft caresses and deep rumble gave her the apology his mouth struggled to form. After his second pass along the delicate column of her throat, he met her eyes and admitted the truth.

"I'm sorry. I knew it wasn't safe. It won't happen again. I'll sleep on the floor."

When worry creased her brow, Quasim strengthened his purr and lulled her into peace.

"Don't move, my prize. Let me take care of you."

Ezmira's lips tilted up in an unexpected smile, causing Quasim's stomach to clench in both worry and desire. Had he damaged her brain, or did she actually enjoy something he said?

His fingers slid over her shoulder as he stood up, and it wasn't until he'd limped to the chest that he realized he'd slipped and called her his prize.

And she'd liked it.

Quasim opened the chest and found the emergency kit. Yanking out the cold pack, he took both back to the bed. After a twist and shake, the long rectangular pack cooled so quickly his fingers went numb before he even set down the emergency kit.

He reached across her and grabbed the blanket he'd left on the other side of the bed and dragged the corner over her neck to shield her skin. She flinched when he settled the cold pack around her throat, but she relaxed almost immediately.

Pushing through the agony in his spine, he stooped over her leg, cleaning it with meticulous care before dabbing on ointment and covering it with a bandage. When he'd finished, he closed the kit, put it back in the chest, then returned to stand beside her.

Quasim's fingers found her face again, and he couldn't pull them away, no matter how hard he tried. He sat on the edge of the bed, ignoring the pain coursing through his own body.

As her eyes focused on him, he fought a grimace and deepened his purr.

He wanted to apologize again but couldn't trust his voice with the ball of emotions lodged in his throat. Her expressive eyes shone with tears as he tried to absorb her pain into himself.

Somehow, his gentle soothing turned bolder, until his palms stroked down her arms and his digits tested the firm muscles under her silky skin. Wanting to take her every ache away, he smoothed his hands over her face and arms again and again, entranced as she relaxed under his care.

When her delicious scent changed to match the throbbing need trapped within his pants, his purr dropped lower than he'd ever rumbled. It took monumental effort, but he pulled his hands away from her.

Despite his best intentions, Quasim couldn't stop his eyes from devouring her tempting form. From the slope of her breasts to the perfect handhold of her hips, he wanted to claim and consume every inch of her.

Which is why he forced himself to stand and walk to the bathroom.

He made sure the curtain closed behind him before he rested his forehead against the wall and sagged in misery.

His world shattered the moment his captors cut the first piece of him away, but Ezmira had flayed him in a more potent way.

His enemies broke him.

She made him want things he could never have.

Turning on the sink, he glanced at the tub and decided he didn't want to soak, even though his entire body was stiff and painful. What he wanted most was to fall under Ezmira's spell. To fly away as her feet danced across the floor. To let the world disappear as she became the center of his attention.

He didn't deserve it.

After splashing cold water on his face, Quasim washed his hands before filling two cups and hobbling to the bed. He sat one on the floor beside it before leaning over his prize.

Ezmira blinked up at him, obviously upset, so he resumed his purr and helped her sit up. The cold pack slid to her lap before he caught it, but he ignored it until she'd sipped down a quarter of the drink. Her face scrunched with each swallow, spearing guilt deeper into his chest.

Not wanting to push her too hard, he guided her shoulders back to the bed and set the cup within reach. His gnarled fingers gathered her hair out from under her torso and smoothed it across the pillow before he stroked her arm.

"So soft."

He caught himself and snatched his hand away from her, remembering the way she'd recoiled when she woke to him petting her in front of the fire.

Ezmira's arm twitched and her brows scrunched together, but Quasim strengthened his purr and swallowed his frustration.

Her pheromones teased him. He knew she couldn't control her body's natural reaction, but in that moment, he wanted to tear her clothes from her and bury his face between her legs.

It was totally inappropriate. She wanted nothing from him but freedom, which he couldn't bear to give her.

He eyed the cold pack resting at the juncture of her thighs and cursed his wayward cock. It pressed against his worn pants, begging to sink inside the soft, luscious female in front of him.

With extreme care, he slid his fingers under the cold pack and ignored the shocks of electricity running up his arm as the backs of his fingers brushed against the fabric separating him from her heat. He knew without a doubt she'd scorch him, leaving a brand so deep he'd never recover, but he'd do everything he could to protect her from himself.

She gasped when his knuckles barely slid along her leggings, making his control waver, but he poured his attention into caring for her. Quasim purred and settled the corner of his blanket and the cold pack back onto her neck before struggling to stand.

His turgid dick, stuck in the confines of his pants, rubbed against the edge of the mattress and stole a hiss from him. His heart thumped a weird staccato as her eyes met his, but he ripped his gaze away and limped to the mantel before he did anything else stupid.

After forcing his agony-filled body to kneel, he stoked the embers and slowly added more kindling until the flames were ready for more. He slid two logs on top before shuffling a few feet away and settling onto his side.

Facing away from the fire, he closed his eyes and gritted his teeth.

The heat from the flames did nothing to ease the tightness in his back, but he shoved away the desire to ask Ezmira for a dance.

She needed rest while he deserved to wallow in misery for a time.

Even though he hadn't meant to hurt her, it was unforgivable, so he laid on the hard floor and counted the seconds as they ticked by, damning himself more with each one.

Chapter 15

Ezmira

It was near impossible to pry her eyes open. While she hadn't expected to sleep again, it appeared she had, though her muscles were still weary.

Pushing up onto her elbows, she checked the furs in front of the fire, but Quasim wasn't there. Hand slipping up to circle her throat, she swallowed painfully as she let her eyes drift around the room in search of him.

She should be terrified of the alpha. She should beg for freedom. Yet with each interaction, her connection grew with this mysterious male who showed the world such a harsh face while his insides screamed for help. He was hurting more than she could even imagine.

Her eyes landed on her bandaged leg. He'd been so regretful and gentle, almost worshipful, when he'd wrapped it. Something warm loosened in her belly, even as confusion tightened her chest.

The curtain to the bathing chamber swished back, Quasim limping through as she sat upright. His eyes caught on hers, searching her face before dropping to her neck. She could see his jaw flex as he clenched his teeth, gaze filled with self-loathing before he turned away.

"Wash up. Do what you need."

Ezmira scrambled from the bed at his rough words, heart aching more than her throat. The pull of the bandage on her leg was more uncomfortable than the actual cut underneath, which made the pain of her heart seem worse somehow. She knew the coldness he showed her wasn't him, his purr the previous night and the haunted look in his eyes were little peeks of the true alpha hidden underneath his scars. He must've been a fierce yet compassionate man before he'd endured whatever unimaginable thing happened to him.

She slipped through the curtain and ensured it was closed all the way behind her before sagging against the wall. The small space was thick with his scent; a shiver ran through her body as it filled her senses.

Raising a hand to her neck once again, she probed with cautious fingers. There was no mirror to check for obvious swelling, and her dark skin wouldn't show anything less than drastic bruising. The flesh was sore when she pressed on it, and it was painful to turn her head or swallow, but it was nothing she couldn't ignore. The guilt on Quasim's face was worse.

After washing up, she stepped out of the bathroom to find the big male kneeling by the fireplace. There was a small pot hanging over the flames, and when he noticed her, he ladled something from it into a mug before getting stiffly to his feet.

"Drink this. It'll help your throat."

She opened her mouth to protest that it wasn't too bad, but all that came out was a harsh garble. Quasim's brow lowered, an angry scowl taking its place over his features as he thrust the mug at her chest. She had no choice but to take it, blinking back a surge of tears.

Settling on the edge of the bed, she gave the contents a cautious sniff before raising the rim to her lips. It was some sort of meat broth, weak, but the warmth helped when she sipped at it.

Quasim came back a moment later, holding out a slice of bread with the crust removed and another piece of cheese. It was the small things he did that told her he wasn't as bad as he seemed, and she had to hide her smile behind the mug as she accepted the offering.

She ate slowly, taking small bites and washing the bread down with the broth, but her throat felt better by the time she finished, and the warmth spreading from her full belly made her feel ready to face the day. She expected Quasim to rush her off to dance as soon as she finished, but he retreated to his chair in the corner, hiding in the shadows of the room. After fidgeting in the silence for a few minutes, she pushed herself to her feet.

"I'm ready if you are."

Her voice was hoarse but steady. She peered toward his corner expectantly, the flames reflecting off his eyes the only thing she could make out. It gave him an eerie look, but she pushed the nerves aside.

"No."

Her breath caught in her throat, the negative response catching her by surprise.

"But..."

She couldn't untangle her thoughts to get any words out, her voice trailing away in her confusion. Quasim rose from his seat, taking a step toward her and wincing with the movement. The hunch of his shoulders showed the agony he was in, so she didn't know why he was denying her. She could help him forget his pain.

"You can't dance. You need to rest."

Her chest clenched, but she forced herself to stand tall and hold his gaze as he moved closer.

"I need to dance. If I don't, my muscles will tighten up and it'll be harder the next time I try. I might end up pulling something and need an even longer recovery time."

Quasim hesitated, the tightness around his eyes and mouth loosening enough to show the fight he was waging within himself. She knew he wanted her to dance, but he was trying not to push her after what happened. There was truth in what she told him, but she needed the escape from reality just as much as he did.

When he seemed frozen with indecision, she turned to the door, hands fumbling with the first of the locks. She made it as high as she could reach before Quasim's scent surrounded her, the heat of his chest pressing against her back to turn the last two locks above her head. It was Ezmira's turn to freeze, her core giving a spasm at the feel of him caging her in.

Skin flushing, she waited, Quasim's hands lingering on the locks. His chest barely brushed against her spine, and she had the strongest urge to lean back and press herself against him. To arch herself so his hips would connect with hers.

The softest rumble began in his chest, but he cut it off before it did more than cause a tingle to run through her. His sudden withdrawal brought a chill to her skin, and it took a moment to get herself under control and move her hand to the knob in front of her.

Resisting the need to look back at him, Ezmira pulled the door open and forced herself to stride down the short hall to her dance space. It wasn't as bright as it had been the day before. The sky beyond the windows was cloudy and turbulent. That was fine—it matched the feelings swirling inside her.

She didn't wait for the music to begin her dance, moving from a simple walk into the flowing forms she used to warm up her muscles before a performance. By the time Quasim crossed the room and wound the music machine, she'd already gotten lost in her own world. A world that now revolved around the male whose presence she couldn't ignore.

Keeping to the beat of the music, she changed the tone from the light, carefree dance she'd done the day before. Her movements were slower, deeper, drawing from the darkness lingering in the corners of the room and from the alpha whose scent danced with her.

She imagined it as a living thing, the other half of the pull and tug within her dance. One that coaxed her closer before scaring her away, only to beg for her return. One that was, at moments, too heavy, but in others, so light it made her feel as if she could soar.

No one had ever affected her the way Quasim did. No one had insinuated themselves so deep within her psyche that she danced just for them, not for herself or her own needs. Beneath the rough, scarred exterior was a noble warrior yearning for a connection he thought he could no longer have. Determination rose within her until her every thought, every shift, even every breath, urged him to believe it was possible. More than anything, she wanted him to realize he still had a life to live.

Pouring everything into her dance, once again she didn't notice the passage of time. She missed the rising heat in her core, ignoring the flutters as mere protests from muscles unused to such extended time dancing.

Instead, she focused on the alpha lingering at the edge of the room, drawing him out until he stood far enough from the wall that she could swirl around him. Teasing him with gentle caresses as she passed, her entire attention set on encouraging him to move with her. To follow the pull of the music and her dance.

A sudden boom and flash of light caused her to stumble, breaking her concentration as her head jerked toward the wall of windows. The gentle grey from when she'd begun had thickened to a swirling blackness, broken only by the lavender lightning crawling across the sky.

For a moment, the fury of the storm mesmerized her before the trembling in her legs brought her back to the present. Realizing Quasim gripped her wrist, she gave him a smile and moved to pull him with her into the next step, but she stumbled again.

She landed heavily against his chest, head spinning. Trying to clear it only left her with fuzzy impressions of light spiking through the darkness, and it took a moment to realize the growl vibrating through her came from the male she rested against and not the skies outside.

Quasim's scent flooded her, bringing more heat to her flesh as her pants grew damp, but it wasn't the only smell pulling at her attention.

"Where are you hurt? The bandage on your leg is still white."

Quasim gripped her shoulders, pushing her away from him as he shook her. Confusion streaked through her until she realized the other scent was blood.

"I-I'm not. I don't know."

Her entire body held a strange combination of numbness and throbbing, the sweat on her brow chilling in the wind barreling through the broken panes. When she tried to step out of his hold, her foot sent a spike of pain up her leg, causing her to wince and fall against him once again as she looked down.

The world spun before a hard shoulder slammed into her stomach. Grunting with the impact, she tried to brace her arms on the rippling muscles under her, but he threw her down onto the bed before she could get a good hold.

"Stupid omega. How did you survive without someone looking after you constantly? Don't you know when to stop?"

She blinked up at him, mind still fuzzy, until the slow throb of pain finally broke through. Quasim gripped her ankle, lifting her foot and showing her the shoe, that had been a pastel yellow, now stained a dark crimson at the toe and heel.

Chapter 16

Quasim

He couldn't hold in his growl as Ezmira shrieked. His fingers weren't gentle enough as he peeled her shoe off her foot, but everything inside him locked in fury.

Words tumbled from his mouth, even though he knew he was the only one to blame.

"Stupid, stupid female. Do you always dance until you bleed?"

Her thick eyelashes swept up and down as she blinked, but he tore his gaze away from her dazed expression and snarled at her bloody foot. She'd danced until blisters burst along her heel where her shoe rubbed it, a large sore oozed from the ball of her foot, and other spots bled from her toes.

The scent of her blood only heightened his fury, but he gentled his movements as he bared her other foot.

It was in the same miserable condition, leaking crimson from worn flesh.

Quasim snarled again and caressed her calves, unable to lift his gaze away from her pain.

"I'm such an idiot. How could I let this happen? I—"

He shut his fool mouth and set to work, giving her calf one last stroke before forcing his wretched body away from her.

After gathering a large bowl, clean water, a washcloth, ointment, and bandages, he sat on the floor at her feet.

He hunched over her, so close he could feel the heat of her legs on his forehead, and slowly lifted one of her feet. When she gasped in pain as he trickled cool water over her toes, he loosened his grip and purred.

Quasim didn't know how long it took, but by the time he finished washing her tiny feet, his back felt as limber as a block of concrete. Not wanting her to get infected, he demanded she stay where she was before he limped to the bathroom sink and lathered his hands.

When he stepped back into the room, he met her eyes and resumed purring. His pupils were most likely as blown as hers since the shock of the situation was too much to remain unaffected.

Her dainty little antlers had curls of green hair twisted this way and that in them from her dancing, and with her colorful clothing, her skin glistened despite its darkness.

He wanted to devour her until neither knew where one ended and the other began, but her fresh wounds grabbed his attention.

It was like a punch to the gut. She'd danced with such grace and beauty he'd lost track of time. She'd never wavered or stepped off tempo despite the blisters on her feet.

He shouldn't have let her dance again, even though he'd wanted it more than his next breath.

Quasim shuffled up to her and framed her face with one of his ugly palms and lost himself in her expression. He wanted to bend down and taste her, but every time he'd done what he wanted, she'd ended up hurt, so he snatched up the ointment and bandages and knelt beside the bed.

He opened the ointment jar and used his fingers to scoop up a large dollop and bent to slather it over every inch of her skin below her right ankle. Her soft sound of relief made his already hard cock pound against his pants. He tortured himself by leaning further, which pinched his partially expanded knot on the seam of his trousers, but also meant he could feel the heat of her thighs on the scarred side of his face.

The gentle caress of her soft fingers on his head startled him.

Quasim snapped his eyes to hers, the purr emanating from his chest dropping an octave without his permission. Ezmira's scent flooded through him, the coppery hint skewing his senses with rage. His hackles rose even as something deep within his psyche screamed at him to run far, far away.

Too bad he couldn't deny his need to see her cared for.

He stretched his left arm up and stroked her chin, watching in fascination as her green irises shrunk further. Ezmira parted her tempting lips as though to speak, but the only sound to pass between them was a whimper.

"Lie back, Ezmira. Let me take care of you," Quasim pleaded.

Her eyes flared in delight before she squinted in confusion, but he urged her shoulder toward the bed and drifted his palm down her arm. Ezmira's fingers captured his wrist as it passed by, but she went lax as his purr seemed to melt her bones.

Exhaustion pulled her into silence as Quasim smeared ointment over her other foot. With deft yet painful movements, he wrapped bandages around both of her feet before carefully lifting her legs and scooting her back on the bed.

When he saw she still watched him with glazed eyes, he fixed her shirt before sliding the blankets over her.

Quasim wanted to crawl under the sheet with her and bury his nose between her glorious breasts, remembering the beads of sweat gathering there. He'd been ridiculously jealous of the salty drops.

Instead of giving in to temptation, Quasim tucked the blanket under her, from her shoulders all the way down her sides, until he propped the excess under her heels.

It wasn't a nest as an omega would make it, but he'd done what he could to make her comfortable.

When he found his fingertips trailing down her face again, he sighed at himself and closed his eyes. Ezmira made a sound of distress, so he pulled his hand away and forced his chest to loosen around his purr.

"Sleep, my prize. I'll fix everything in the morning."

The moment Ezmira's breathing morphed to the slow cadence of sleep, Quasim opened his eyes and stared down at her. He studied her matted hair spanned across the pillow, the curls tangled in her antlers, and the exhaustion pulling her delicate features tight. His fingers sought her cheek again, and without his permission, they traced the side of her face and kept moving lower until he could feel the flutter of her heartbeat near the base of her neck.

Unease crept through him.

Her heart shouldn't be racing, yet it pulsed as though she still leaped across the dance floor. His stomach tightened as he realized she felt hotter than before, like her flesh was trying to scorch him for daring to touch her.

Was she sick? Had he pushed her beyond her endurance and allowed an illness to sneak in?

The truth hung just out of reach. His mind failed him. He couldn't understand.

There was no enemy to hunt down and slay. He'd bandaged her wounds and tucked her in like a child, cocooning her scent away in a mock nest.

Quasim needed to watch her dance again but refused to let her until she rested and healed. He couldn't keep allowing her to be hurt.

As worry gnawed at his stomach, Quasim turned and limped to the door. He unlocked it and slipped out, knowing Ezmira was too tired to wake on her own.

He needed fresh air to clear his mind. The bedchamber was too full of pheromones for him to think rationally.

After hobbling down the hallway, he stood in the entrance to the old ballroom and perused the space. Even with crumbling plaster and broken windows, it still held a regal ambiance—the thick lines and ornate details lent a majestic air—but his usual sense of sanctuary did not rise.

Quasim forced his aching body down the length of the dance hall, letting the peace of remembering Ezmira's graceful movements carry him forward. He unlocked one of the double doors and went out onto the balcony before shutting it behind him. The storm had blown itself out, leaving everything shiny in its wake.

Laying a gnarled hand on the crumbling railing, he recalled Ezmira's terror at the height and his horrible behavior.

She didn't belong here.

He didn't deserve her.

His heart sunk into his toes, but he knew it was for the best. Now he had memories of her lithe body and colorful clothing whipping across his ballroom. He could cling to those.

It hurt him, but he had to let her go. He must return her to her troupe.

He was an idiot for taking her and, even worse, for being so cruel when she didn't deserve it.

Raising his chin to the moon, he sucked in a few calming breaths before turning back into his sanctuary. Following his instincts, he double checked that the lock was secure before stalking across Ezmira's dance hall. Bone ground against bone as his knee struggled to support his weight, but he closed the bedchamber door behind him and systematically turned every lock.

He swallowed the sorrow building in his throat when he remembered the silent, intimate moment of having her between him and the door. He'd felt connected to her in that moment, but all she'd wanted was to escape into her dance.

When he turned and found Ezmira in the exact position he'd left her, Quasim filled his lungs with what should have been a calming breath.

His senses went haywire.

The floral, fruity pheromones clouding the air burst into his nostrils and sent molten lava coursing down his decrepit spine.

Ezmira was in estrous. His subconscious had told him, but he'd refused to recognize the signs. He'd focused too much on her wounds.

An omega's heat was a force of its own, stealing all higher thinking and stripping both alpha and omega to their base instincts. They lasted for weeks unless tended by an alpha's knot, and while she didn't need a claiming mark, it took a strong-willed alpha. He wasn't sure he could hold back, not with the lithe and luscious Ezmira.

The urge to rut and claim the amazing omega resting in his sheets drove his feet forward.

His grinding knee and ruined back stopped him. The scarred stumps on his back screaming in pain highlighted his shortcomings.

Quasim would never be fit for mating, especially not for Ezmira. She was too kind, too delicate, and too graceful to be shackled to a broken alpha like him. She had the chance to travel through the galaxies while he remained trapped in a cell of his own making.

Two steps would clear the distance between him and the tempting female before him, but he couldn't take them. He wanted to stroke her hair and feel the silky softness of her skin again, but he kept his talons in place.

What he needed to do was turn and leave the room.

Her eyes popped open and destroyed his ability to retreat.

Chapter 17

Ezmira

Lava burned through her veins, the light blanket that had once been too little to keep her warm now causing her to break out in sweat.

Or maybe it was the grey eyes peering into hers.

Quasim's shocked expression was the first she'd seen where he didn't seem to hold back, but torn desire quickly followed. The alpha wanted her.

But he also wanted to run.

Struggling from the blanket, the throbbing in her feet was a distant concern, easily flicked away. She rolled to her knees on the mattress, holding out a hand to the male who seemed frozen in place.

"Quasim—"

She'd barely said his name when his expression slammed closed, the anger written on his features causing her to recoil with a gasp.

"No!"

He turned away but didn't seem able to force himself to leave the side of the bed. Clutching one hand to her lower belly as a cramp pulled at the muscles, she rose to her knees once again. Reaching out her shaking hand, she gently laid it on his shoulder, the skin twitching under her palm.

She couldn't resist giving him a light caress. It wasn't just that her heat had come, her instincts had drawn her to him from the moment she'd awoken in his den.

"Please, Quasim. It won't end without you. I'll be in pain for weeks."

She let her tears fill her voice. She didn't want him to think she wanted him because he was the only alpha available who could stop her heat, but she knew he wouldn't accept that she truly wanted *him*. Quasim had proven he was a good man and alpha under the influence of his pain, and if she could give him pleasure by enjoying her body, she was glad to let him have her.

"I need you."

He trembled under her soft touch, hands balled at his sides. His head hung, shoulders heaving with the deep breaths he was taking.

Another cramp tore through her middle, pulling a gasp from her lips as she hunched forward. Dark eyes turned to meet hers, the grey a thin ring around his blown pupils.

"I will not claim you."

The gritted words seemed more meant for himself than her, but Ezmira nodded her understanding. It had been reassuring from previous alphas who'd helped her through her heat, but she felt an odd twinge of regret at his words. It was hard for an alpha to resist claiming an omega when they helped them through a cycle, but it wasn't impossible, and she knew Quasim's control was better than most.

She trusted him.

When he stepped away from her and slipped from beneath her hand, she let out a groan, but he stopped at the trunk against the wall and began digging through it. Coming back to her with the last of the bread and cheese, he pressed them into her hands, despite Ezmira trying to shove it away.

"Eat. Now."

Tears trembled in her lashes and her stomach revolted at the thought of forcing the food down, but she sucked in a shaky breath and nodded again. Settling onto her bottom, she lifted the cheese to her lips as Quasim disappeared into the bathing room, taking a nibble as she tried to breathe through the rising need burning her.

He returned a moment later with a full cup of water and a pile of fabric over one arm. Confusion drifted through her splintered thoughts until he dropped it beside her and she realized it was his clothing. There were no soft fluffy things here, but he was trying to supply her with nesting material, and her heart clenched.

She reached out for the shirt on top, but Quasim's hand pinned it in place as he let out a low growl. Tipping her gaze up to meet his as her brow furrowed, she shivered at the look in his eye.

"Not until you eat."

Swallowing hard, she raised the cheese to her lips and forced herself to bite and chew until she'd eaten the small block. When she gave him a hopeful look, he reached out and tapped the bread resting in the hand on her lap, and she let out a sigh before choking it down as well.

She was sweating freely by the time she finished, her pants clinging to her because of the slick seeping from her core with each cramp. The intensity was growing, and she knew it wouldn't be long before she was writhing in pain and incapable of thinking.

As soon as her hand was empty of food, Quasim pressed the cup into her palm.

"All of it."

His growl forced another cramp, a whimper slipping through her lips as she tried to comply with his order. Her hand shook so much she almost sloshed water over the side, so he kept his grip on the cup and helped her bring it to her lips.

The moment the liquid hit her tongue, she sucked it down with relish, her body knowing it needed the fluid to get through what was coming. When she finished the first and he pushed another cup to her lips, she didn't complain, gazing up at him as she drank down the contents of it as well.

The vibration that came from him when he took away the empty glass melted the tension in her muscles, making her want to press herself against him to get more of it, but he moved out of reach. Setting the cups on top of the dresser, he faced her and crossed his arms over his chest but didn't return to his place before her. Confused, Ezmira moved to reach for him, but the blanket under her hand caught her attention.

That would not do.

With a disgusted growl rising from her chest, she rolled off the bed and yanked the offending blanket from the mattress. The action sent the rest of the items on the bed scattering across the floor, but it didn't matter. She needed a clean slate to fix the mess that had been there.

Stooping to feel through the fabrics available, she let out an unhappy whimper. The softest items were too small to cover the nest, and there wasn't enough to make a comfortable layer to sink into. She lifted an odd shape of material and scrunched her brows, unable to figure out what she held until the two distinct holes told her it was a shirt, ripped straight down the middle. After dropping it back onto the floor, she looked around. Spotting a few more items by the fire, she snatched those up to add to her pile. The only good thing about all of them was the scent rising to tickle her nose.

With so few to choose from, she had to use what was available, so she selected the most offending texture to layer on the mattress first. Irritated snarls fell from her lips as she worked each piece into her creation, the purr rising from behind her doing little to soothe her temper.

She was halfway through the pile of fabric when the feelings overflowed and she went into a rage. Screeching and throwing fabrics, she dismantled the partial nest, rending the worst of the blankets in half until a large hand tangled in her locks. Bowed backward, her chest rose and fell in great heaves as she looked up at the snarling alpha, his fierceness drowning out her own.

"Calm yourself."

The words were rough, and the gentle shake he gave her pulled at her scalp and peaked her nipples. Distracted by the sight of his bare chest and the scent rolling over her, her own complaints melted away as another cramp caused fresh slick to soak her pants.

The alpha dragged her off the bed before pushing her back toward it as he released her hair. Turning desperate eyes to the big male who once again put space between them, despair rose in her chest.

"Begin again."

Swallowing her sob, Ezmira turned back to the bed. Her pants were sticky and irritating when she moved to climb onto the mattress again, so she paused and peeled them off, followed by her top. She was still hot, but at least the fabric no longer constricted her.

Rubbing the soft material of her dress between her fingers, an idea formed, and she reached for the blankets once again. She usually created nests she could disappear inside of, but she didn't have the proper sized items to use, and the room was already uncomfortably warm.

She cast a glance over her shoulder at Quasim. He stood with his legs braced wide and his arms crossed over his scarred chest as his fingers bit into his bunched biceps. The hunger apparent on his face sent a fresh wave of slick to wet her thighs, and she couldn't help raising her bottom to draw her alpha's attention.

His rough growl met her action, bringing a smirk to her lips as she turned back to her nest. Her alpha didn't need a top sheet to cover the nest—it would only irritate the injuries on his back. He would be her cover, protecting her from the world.

It didn't take long after she'd decided. She added the softest shirts to the top layer with her dress and the pants he'd given her. Sitting back on her feet, she surveyed the nest she'd created. It was small and not as bright as she'd usually make, but it was enough.

Turning to the alpha still watching her, Ezmira ducked her head, suddenly shy. Quasim had chosen her for her dancing, because she could soothe his pain away for a time, and while he'd been as caring toward her as he was capable, she didn't know if he truly wanted her.

She sucked in a deep breath before raising her head to meet his gaze again. The tightness around his eyes and mouth were still there, showing his pain, though hunger warred with it. Glancing down at the pants slung low on his hips, she could see the evidence of his desire pressing against the fabric, and the scent of his excitement filled her nostrils.

Holding out her hand to him, she watched as he struggled to let himself move closer. When he still stopped a few paces from the bed, she slid over the edge and closed the space between them.

"I need you, Quasim. Help me? Please?"

Letting her fingers skim the top of his pants, she felt him shudder as her hands met over the clasp. Holding his gaze, she released the fabric, the heat of his erection almost burning her when her fingers dipped to circle his trapped girth.

Quasim hissed, hands fisting at his sides as she explored his length. His tip felt almost dangerously sharp with its distinct point, and shifting her fingers lower allowed her to explore the flared, blunt crown of his head. Wedging her hand even further into his pants, her eyes widened as she encountered ridges along the sides of his shaft. Her breath caught on a moan as she imagined the way they would feel inside her.

When he still refused to move, Ezmira released his hot flesh and took hold of his pants, pushing them down and planting a kiss on his head as it bobbed in front of her, testing the soft skin over the intimidating tip. The slight fear she'd felt over seeing his impressive size melted away as his heat seeped into her lips. Standing and turning her back on the big male, she let her hips sway as she climbed back into her nest, keeping her knees parted and her bottom up as she leaned forward and pressed her chest to the bed. Pushing out the loudest purr she could manage, she glanced over her shoulder and waited.

"Please, alpha."

Her plea caused his control to snap, and Quasim surged onto the bed behind her. Clenching her eyes shut and bracing for the thrust she expected to follow, she gasped in surprise when his tongue swiped up her inner thigh. Moaning into the bedding, she canted her hips higher to give him better access to her core, but after just a few quick, hot flicks, his grip on her hips tightened and he moved to kneel behind her.

"Can't wait."

His gasp heightened her own need, her core throbbing as she waited for his invasion. She felt the scorching tip of him at her opening and pressed backward, tightening her grip on the bed.

Chapter 18

Quasim

His hips thrust forward and buried the swollen tip of his cock in her tight heat. With the taste of her slick lingering on his tongue and the visual delight she'd already gifted him, Quasim fought for control.

Her yelp filled a part of his soul. Even though she made little sounds of discomfort, she pushed back, seeking more of him. He surged deeper into her and groaned as she clamped around him.

With her ass up in the air and her breasts flattened by the bed, she was a sensual sight he'd never forget.

Scorching electricity ran up from his ridges as slick gushed around him, and her needy cries carried the sparks straight into his heart.

How had she become so dear to him in such a short amount of time?

Quasim ground his teeth together, ignoring the urge to lean down and fill his mouth with her midnight flesh and bite.

She could never be his. He'd help her through this heat, nothing more. All she needed was his knot lodged deep inside her. Then she'd be free to go back to her troupe.

He reached forward, another groan joining his deep purr as he invaded her further, but he held her hip with one hand so she couldn't drop deeper onto his cock. Quasim brushed the strands of vibrant green hair off the side of her face, needing to watch her expression as he plundered her depths.

Half of Ezmira's face hid in her nest, and even though pride surged through him at the bliss and need warring within her features, it wasn't enough.

He wanted to see every nuance of thought and sensation crossing her gorgeous green eyes as he satisfied her heat. He longed to watch her swollen lips part on every gasp and mewl as he ruined her. He needed to own her in every way except the one that would force her to be with him forever.

Quasim caught her hair in his fist and pushed her head into the nest, preparing for her shrieks as he pulled his cock away.

Her fury spiked when he left her tight, warm sheath, but he kept her scalp pinned as he reached under her and grabbed her opposite hip.

Quasim's spine screamed in agony as he flipped her, the movement requiring him to lift and twist, but only enough that her shoulder scraped along the bed before she was settled on her on her back.

His purr faltered as Ezmira's nails scratched down his abs, the streak of sharp pain colliding with his agony and splintering his hold on reality.

The second he released her hair, Ezmira pierced him with a pleading look.

He wrapped his gnarled fingers around her hips and dragged her toward him.

Before her searching fingers touched his cock, he fitted his tip to her entrance and thrust inside.

Ezmira's chin flew up as his thick shaft barreled into her; his tapered tip reaching the soft, spongy spot at the front and his ridges stimulating the walls of her channel.

His snarl snapped her attention to his face.

"Look at me."

Whatever she saw in his expression made her melt under him until he snapped his hips forward and crammed more of himself into her. Her mouth popped open on a gasp as the start of his semi-inflated knot stretched her entrance.

"Please, Quasim. More."

Her usual high, clear voice vibrated with desire, and he lost his control as his name formed on her lips. With a brutal thrust, he pulled her flush against him, barreling so deep into her neither could form words.

Her slick drenched their thighs and soaked the nest under them as he set a punishing rhythm. Pain speared into him from his stumps, but he refused to slow. The bliss of taking her drowned out everything else.

Quasim bared his teeth and growled, watching as Ezmira's entire body seized. Her mouth opened on a silent scream as he thrust into her again and again, keeping her locked in pleasure for long, soul-shattering seconds.

As with her dance, she stole his pain and whisked it away, filling him with awe. She sucked in huge gasps of air as she tried to recover, and he held himself still solely so he could watch her orgasm again.

Her soaked folds wrapped around his shaft, teasing the slope of his knot as her trembling insides massaged his tip.

Quasim couldn't force his mouth to form words, so he demanded her attention with a snarl.

Blown pupils framed by flushed cheekbones and matted green hair filled his vision.

The second she regained her breath, her womb clamped down, and she whined through her gritted teeth. Her body warmed further, and a wave of slick gushed from her depths as her heat flared back to life with a vengeance.

Quasim filled his palm with her breast and kneaded the mound, moaning with her at the feel of her tight nipple rubbing against him.

She writhed against the ruined nest and pleaded for relief with her eyes. He enjoyed the sight but hated knowing he could have ended her suffering if he wasn't such a greedy bastard.

The vulnerability in her expression made him want to shield her away from the world, which only reinforced that he hadn't supplied her with enough nesting material. Unable to deny either of them for another second longer, he released her glorious breast and leaned over her. With one forearm braced beside her shoulder, he latched on to her hip with his other hand and drove himself deep into her.

His spine screamed in agony over the position, but only the apocalypse would stop him.

As she tightened around him again, his knot expanded, and liquid fire shot from his groin and burst through his shaft. Before he seated his rapidly growing knot behind her pubic bone,

Ezmira squealed, clamped her slim fingers around his biceps, and bit his pectoral.

Shock made him yank his hips away, his ballooning knot popping free of her entrance.

Her moan of ecstasy pulled molten lava from him, and his hips thrust forward, mashing the thick part of his shaft against her pussy lips as he released his seed into her womb, his knot angry at being denied entrance back into her constrictive heat.

He dropped his other forearm to the bed and bracketed her head with his hands, locked in uncertainty. Ezmira gave a sloppy lick to the wound her teeth had caused before falling limp under him. Every muscle in her body relaxed.

Quasim guided her head to the bed and studied her face. With each of her steady, exhausted breaths, his panic grew.

She'd marked him.

He knew she hadn't meant to.

Quasim yanked his cock out of her and stumbled from the bed.

This was wrong. He should have protected her better, kept her facing away from him, but he'd given in to his selfish desires and turned her so he could see all of her.

She deserved so much better.

With his heart as brittle as the mangled bones protruding from the stumps on his back, he cradled Ezmira to his chest and carried her to the bath. After sitting in the basin, he turned on the water and washed every inch of her, worshipping her with every stroke and hating himself more with every second he forced her to endure his presence.

Even deep in exhausted slumber, she shouldn't have to deal with his stupidity.

The slide of her silky skin against his etched into his memory, for even though he said goodbye with every touch, he eagerly stored it all away. He'd have to hope their coupling was enough to break her heat.

Once washed of every trace of their mating, Quasim lifted her from the bath and carefully hobbled to the bed. Standing over the sad excuse for a nest, he gritted his teeth. She'd even had to use her new clothes, which meant he had nothing clean to wrap her in.

Pushing everything to the other side of the mattress, he settled her onto the bed and stopped himself from caressing her face.

He needed to do the right thing for once, no matter how much it hurt.

Gathering the dirty materials, he took them to the bath and scrubbed her clothes and what he needed to wear for the night's outing. The second he finished, he hung them over the furniture closest to the mantel and stoked the fire. It jumped to life with ease, almost as though it sensed the turmoil in his soul and wished to escape his ire.

He stood over Ezmira and watched the rise and fall of her chest. His heart ached, more so than the bite mark over it, but as he brooded over his prize, an odd peace settled over him. Quasim knew fate didn't want him happy, and he finally had an excuse to quit fighting.

This way, at least *she* could be happy. He could say he'd done one semi-righteous thing in his lifetime, even if he was the one to create the circumstances.

He pulled his clothing on while it was still damp but waited until hers were warm and dry before dressing her. The entire time, she lay limp like a rag doll, so tired she didn't respond to his ministrations. A few times, he stopped to check her vitals and was relieved when they were normal.

As her leg twitched when he began inspecting the scabbed wounds on her feet, he retrieved a vial and syringe from the chest. He'd used the medication when the nightmares were too powerful to escape from, but he couldn't resist sleep any longer. It was strong enough to keep Ezmira out until he'd completed his plan.

He sat on the edge of the mattress, using the firelight to ensure he put the proper amount of sedative in the syringe before cleaning the crook of her arm.

Ezmira's eyes opened. She gave him a dreamy smile before he inserted the needle.

Her brows scrunched as she let out a whimper before her eyelids swept down again.

Allowing himself one more caress of her face, he put the medicine away and retrieved ointment and bandages. He longed to linger over wrapping her feet again but pushed away the desire and cared for her as quickly as he could.

After gingerly sliding her slippers onto her feet, he snuffed out the fire and prepared to leave.

In the dark, he disengaged every lock on the door before limping back to the mattress.

Picking up the sweet little omega lying in his bed, he ignored the part of his soul screaming in distress and kissed the top of her head.

His prize would live a long and happy life. Far away from him and his selfish needs.

He shuffled her around until her knees bracketed his waist and her head laid on his chest. Using his most sturdy straps, he fashioned a harness around the both of them until she stayed flush against his front.

No matter what he did, the straps rubbed against his stumps, but he didn't care.

Nothing could compare to the gaping hole in his heart.

She may have arrived slung over his shoulder like a sack of potatoes, but she sure as hell wouldn't leave that way. He'd do anything to treat her like the precious treasure she was.

After throwing his cloak over his shoulders, he opened the bedchamber door.

With sure yet agonizing movements, he left his sanctuary, locking the balcony doors behind him. A misplaced surge of gratitude washed over him as he looked over the side and recalled her initial reaction to standing out here.

At least he could save her from having to scale the outside of the building while conscious.

Halfway down the path, his thighs burned and his fingers threatened to lose their purchase on the crumbling siding. The past few days landed on his shoulders with a heavy thump, weighing him down, but he gritted his teeth and forced his aching body to continue. Just knowing she depended on him gave him the strength he needed.

His talons scratched along the marble stairs as he hobbled down the last flight, each lift of his leg more difficult than the last.

He didn't want to let Ezmira go, but he knew he had to.

The wind whipped around him as he limped down the street toward where he'd hidden his ship, so he pulled his cloak around him and hid his prize from the gloom.

No, not his prize. Not anymore.

He had to do everything he could to save her.

Even if that meant giving her up.

***

Quasim battled over which location was safest for her. In the end, there was only one logical place. He'd stolen her from there, so he should return her there.

The palace gardens were embarrassingly easy to infiltrate, even for a decrepit alpha like him, although maybe that was because he'd grown up on the premises. He knew the guard's schedule and the easiest way to slip over the fence.

Quasim had full faith that Armyn would see to Ezmira's safety. It helped to know that his brother-in-arms and prince had already found his mate and would have no interest in claiming Ezmira for himself.

She looked so peaceful, lying amid the soft grass, even more beautiful than the blooming flowers.

Her hair proved silkier than the bed of blossoms he'd settled her into.

Despite telling himself he had to let her go, Quasim stroked her vibrant green locks and caressed her face. Either a palace worker or the royal family would find her. He should be far away, but he needed a few more moments.

A drop of water landed on her neck, startling him into searching their surroundings.

No one was around. It hadn't rained in days. The trees overhead showed no signs of moisture.

Another drop landed next to the first.

A strangled sound left his throat as he realized they were his tears.

Through the violence of torture and the turmoil of coming to terms with his new reality, he'd never once shed a single tear, yet for the tiny, gentle omega, he cried.

He needed her.

He didn't deserve her.

She was better off without him. He never should have kidnapped her.

More salty liquid dropped onto her vulnerable throat, tempting him to bury his face there, but he knew he couldn't trust himself. He'd bite her out of his own selfish need.

After one final stroke of her hair and cheek, Quasim wiped his tears off her with his cloak, fanned her colorful clothing over the grass, and turned away.

Chapter 19

Ezmira

The chill of the wind on her skin roused her, but it was the birds chirping that had her bolting upright. There'd been no animal noises in Quasim's hideaway, nor the sound of rustling leaves and flowing water.

Ezmira had to scrub her eyes to get them open, grit trying to glue them shut. Her body begged her to crawl to the stream she could hear nearby, but she did not know why she was outside.

Where was Quasim?

Dew soaked into her pants where she knelt in the grass, trying to figure out where she was. The bushes on three sides and trees beyond the stream blocked her view of anything else, but the space seemed familiar.

Voices nearby caught her attention, and she turned her head toward them just as two women stepped through an opening in the surrounding hedge. They froze, staring back at her with the same surprise Ezmira knew she had written all over her face.

The smaller of the two, the one with delicate glass-like wings, came rushing over after her moment of surprise. Ezmira recognized her from the ball… however many days ago it was.

"Are you okay?"

Ezmira swallowed, her throat still painful from the night of Quasim's nightmare, not sure how to answer the question. She felt weak and dehydrated, but it was nothing worse than how she usually felt after her heat. The painful pulling in her chest caused the worst distress, so she raised a hand to rub at the spot.

"I-I think so."

Her voice was a rough rasp that caused her to wince. When Ezmira tried to get to her feet, she wobbled, and the smaller woman stepped forward to wrap an arm around her. The first breath she took had pale blue eyes flashing back up to Ezmira's.

"Are you going into heat? Do I need to get you somewhere? Call someone?"

Her low hiss held the urgency Ezmira felt, but Ezmira shook her head at the questions.

"Not starting. Ending. Where's Quasim?"

The other woman's brows lowered.

"Quasim left during the ball. He hasn't stayed here since before he joined the military with Armyn."

She continued to study Ezmira, her eyes widening after a moment.

"You're the dancer! The one who disappeared. Your troupe has been looking for you! What happened? How did you end up here?"

Ezmira's head spun, causing her to stumble and almost fall, which would have taken the little Fayrie down with her. Her hand trembled when she raised it to her head, the pain in her chest growing.

"I-I don't know. I was with Quasim. I need to find him."

She tried to straighten, but the other woman refused to release her. Ezmira was grateful for the support, but the fluttering inside her rib cage demanded she pull herself together and find her missing alpha.

"Come, let me help you. Armyn will know if Quasim returned and where to find him."

Fighting the urge to resist, Ezmira nodded, letting the woman turn her toward the palace rising above the gardens. It seemed like it had been such a long time since the night she stepped out to have a moment to herself, only to be taken by Quasim.

She'd wanted nothing more than to escape, yet now that he'd apparently released her, she only wanted to find him again. What happened during her heats was always fuzzy, but she knew he'd tended to her. He'd been ruthless while giving her body exactly what it needed, despite the pain it had likely caused him.

And if the pulsing in her chest was anything to go by, she'd claimed him.

It was hard to ignore the pain of rejection at knowing he hadn't marked her in return. There was no discomfort in her neck or shoulder where his bite should have bound them, only the frantic beating inside her ribs of a half-formed link searching for the piece that would make it complete.

If he truly didn't want her, she would live with the consequences, but Ezmira needed to find him and hear it from his lips. She had a sick feeling in her gut that dumping her at the palace was his way of saving her again, and he was about to do something stupid.

She barely paid attention to where the female led her, accepting a glass of water that was pressed into her hands but otherwise keeping her head down and focused on taking the next step. It seemed like they'd walked for miles before delicate hands guided her to sit in a plush chair.

A quick look showed her she was in an office. The size and luxury left no doubt that it was Prince Armyn's. Taking another look at the woman who had helped her, Ezmira realized why she recognized her.

"Thank you, Princess. I don't mean to impose," she said as she tried to struggle out of the seat, but small fingers on her shoulder held her down. Cinza colored when Ezmira called her princess, and the small smile she shot at Ezmira was self-conscious.

"I'm not a princess yet. The wedding is still a month away."

She took a breath before straightening and patting Ezmira's shoulder.

"Just stay right here while I find Armyn. It's no problem. Quasim is his friend, and he will want to help if this involves him."

Nodding, Ezmira let her body sag into the cushions. Sipping the water, her eyes drifted closed as she tried to remember what happened. The last thing she recalled was being in Quasim's arms, the taste of copper flooding her mouth as her teeth sank into the meat above his heart.

Tears pricked at the backs of her eyes, a sob catching in her chest and threatening to send her spiraling. Even half-finished, the bond connected them together, and she knew the dread she felt was because he'd left her. She only hoped the underlying worry was her imagination and not something more.

"You've been with Quasim?"

The tall male striding into the room wasted no time with pleasantries, launching into his question before he'd cleared the door. He took a few steps further into the room, with Cinza following close on his heels, before he stopped as if he'd slammed into a wall. Nostrils flaring, he looked her up and down as his expression turned calculating.

"Y-Yes. Since the ball."

"How did you get here?"

The imperial tone still filled his voice, though he kept his distance and pulled Cinza against his side. His grip on her looked tight, distracting Ezmira for a moment with the thought that the larger male would hurt the tiny Fayrie by accident.

"I-I don't know. I was with Quasim. I danced for him and went into heat and he... I—"

Demanding words cut her off before she could stumble through any more of her explanation.

"Did he claim you?"

Ezmira's mouth still hung open, the question freezing the air in her lungs. Her hesitance appeared to override the alpha's desire to keep away from her, because in two steps, he stood beside her. Gripping her hair in one massive paw, he tilted her head each way before dropping it as if burned and backing away.

"I don't see any marks, and you still haven't explained why you were in my palace gardens."

The prince's expression darkened. Ezmira's lip trembled with the tears she tried to hold back.

"He didn't claim me. I…"

She had to stop and suck in a breath before she could force the words from her lips. Dropping her gaze to her hands resting in her lap, she continued.

"I claimed him, and then I woke up here. Alone."

The last word was a mere whisper, but the ache in her soul was a screaming pain she didn't think she would survive.

Trying to ignore the panic growing in her chest, she risked a peek at the couple standing across the room. The grin spread across the alpha's face was confusing enough to distract her from her misery.

"That's the best thing I've heard since Cinza was screaming on my knot this morning."

Eyes darting to the little female by his side, Ezmira watched Cinza's cheeks flush pink as she slapped the prince's arm and let out a hiss. Brows rising, Ezmira turned her attention back to Armyn for clarification.

"If he's earned your claim, he must be doing better. Did he come back with you? Where is he? Why didn't he finish claiming you before returning?"

He shot the questions at her too fast for her to respond. Striding around the desk Ezmira sat at, Armyn dropped into the chair across from her and pulled Cinza into his lap, tucking her against him and letting out a soft purr. As quiet as it was, and despite coming from another male, the sound helped loosen the bands twisted around Ezmira's chest so she could speak.

"I don't think he's here. The pain..."

She raised a hand to her chest, rubbing the spot that throbbed with each beat of her heart. The one that told her the male she'd claimed had left her.

"I don't think he wants me."

The humiliating confession brought fresh tears to her eyes. Trying to turn away from her shame, pale blue irises, intense even amid Armyn's hold, caught her attention. Only the growl that followed shook her free and pulled her attention back up.

"Damned idiot. Fool thinks he's cursed to suffer forever. I doubt he doesn't want you, but his misplaced sense of self-loathing may have driven him to deny you."

The growl laced through the prince's words sent a shiver down Ezmira's spine.

"There's no way to break a bond, even a half-complete one. He knows that, and he knows it'll cause you pain as long as he lives. He wouldn't hurt you like that, so why would he—"

Armyn's voice trailed off, his eyes widening in alarm even as Ezmira felt hers do the same. He must have come to the same conclusion she had; that Quasim was planning on breaking the bond the only way he could.

With his death.

Armyn surged to his talons, Cinza letting out a startled squeak before he placed her on her feet at his side. Leaning over the desk, he planted his hands on the surface and focused his ferocious gaze on Ezmira.

"Where did you go with him?"

"I don't know! I just woke up there."

Fear flooded through her veins, her heart beating so fast it felt like it was trying to escape her chest. She had to stop Quasim, but she didn't know the planet well enough to even give the prince a direction. More words burst from her chest, but her memory felt jumbled and incomplete.

"He said the name of the city, but I-I can't remember."

"Were there windows? Did you look outside?"

Trying to focus, Ezmira swallowed and thought back to her one trip outside the three rooms Quasim had kept her in.

"We were in a building, high up. There was a balcony. Everything was crumbling, old, worn down. Some buildings around us had collapsed. There was no power…"

She trailed off as Armyn straightened.

"Cryptik. That shithole is the only place so derelict with people still living in it."

"Please! We have to find him."

Her stomach clenched, expecting the alpha to deny her, but his eyes softened as he stared down at her.

"We will. If anyone can stop him, it'll be you. I need you to save my friend."

Ezmira's chest tightened, but she nodded. She would do whatever it took, even if it meant living with the pain coiled inside her. Despite the way they met, she knew Quasim was a good man, and he didn't deserve what had happened to him. Even if he didn't want to be bonded, he didn't have to give up his life just to end her pain.

Chapter 20

Quasim

His body seized as he landed on his forearms on the balcony floor, the trip up the side of the building too draining for him to land on his talons.

Quasim knew there was no relief for him, but he sucked in great lungfuls of oxygen, hoping to settle his pounding heart.

Crimson slid down the inside of his left bicep, the position making her claiming mark ooze. Ezmira had tried to lick him and close the wound she'd made, but his feathers had blocked her tongue from reaching the outer corner. Plus, she'd been so exhausted, she'd barely managed a quick swipe before she fell asleep. He shook his head but only scrambled his brain.

If a half-formed bond was hell on the one who did the biting, and he was only catching a portion of her pain, then he was an even bigger asshole than he'd thought.

Forcing his exhausted body upright, he looked over the railing and surveyed the crumbling city. The Gothic style matched the heaviness of his heart, as did the decay infecting everywhere he looked.

Turning away from the cityscape, he unlocked one of the double doors to his sanctuary and stepped inside. Not bothering to even shut the door behind him, he limped to the wall with the murals and ran his fingertips over the fading surface as he slowly made his way to the other end of the large room. Each step brought him memories of Ezmira's full skirt coloring the drab space and her slim legs carrying her across the marble.

When he reached the music player, he grabbed the lever and cranked it, ignoring the jabbing pain from his shoulders.

A slow trail of wet warmth trickled down from his right stump. The harness he'd carried Ezmira away in had opened the frail skin between his thick scars, but he didn't care.

With every beat of his heart, his world shrank a little further. He knew what he had to do to save the sweet little omega who'd stolen his soul long before she'd sunk her teeth into his flesh.

Quasim released the lever and flipped the switch, waiting until the music filled the dance hall before he turned toward the hallway.

His uneven gait carried him to the open bedchamber, and for a moment he stood looking through the doorframe. Bittersweet emotions rolled through him as their mingled pheromones leaked from the room where they'd shared such intense intimacy.

He stepped through the door and skimmed his fingers over the mantel on his way to the chair in the corner. Staring down at the faded fabric, he recalled sitting there and watching her waking for the first time, the sass she'd given despite her inherent sweetness.

She'd been terrified, but he hadn't cared. He'd naively thought he could handle whatever arose, so long as she danced for him. Anything was worth it to take the pain away.

Before he turned away, Quasim pulled his cloak over his head and tossed it into the chair.

He hobbled to the bathroom and brushed his palms across the tub's lip, wishing it were her silky flesh under his hands. The soaked bedding still floated in the cold water, but he wasn't worried about having clean bedding anymore.

Shuffling back through the curtain to the bedchamber, he took the last apple from the dresser and stood by the mantel. Quasim couldn't bring himself to bite into the red orb any more than he could turn toward the bed. He knew neither would give him what he craved.

The ash in the fireplace shifted as a gust of wind blew over the top of the chimney. Even with the door's solid weight, it knocked against the wall as the same wind stole through the broken glass in the dance hall and battered the hallway.

After filling his lungs with a fortifying breath, he squeezed the apple in his fist and faced the bed.

The bare mattress wafted the faint scent of Ezmira's pheromones to his nostrils, but other than that, no trace of her remained. It hurt to know he'd never see her again, but he stretched his decrepit body to its full height and grit his teeth.

He'd smashed the apple without meaning to, just how he'd destroyed Ezmira's feet. Juice dripped from the pulp in his hand.

The odd numbness creeping along his senses burst, filling him with despair. Without conscious thought, he flung the crushed apple across the room and roared.

There was only one way to give Ezmira the peace she deserved.

He had to end her suffering by ending his life.

Flinging the sticky residue onto the floor with the flick of his arm, he snarled and stalked into the hall. He ignored the turmoil in his chest and stomped into the ballroom, using the beat of the music to carry him across the large space. His right leg dragged with every step, the bones in his knee refusing to move. His blood ran cold, the coagulating mess running down from his shoulder and her bite mark chilling with his thoughts.

He'd refused to think of flying since his enemies had stolen his wings. With her dance, Ezmira had given him the freedom to soar among the clouds once again.

Now he'd fly one last time.

The second he flung the swinging double doors out of his way, he stopped in his tracks.

Ezmira stood like a colorful statue in the middle of the balcony, her wide eyes showcasing both her fear of heights and the pain of their half-formed bond. Quasim's heart leaped forward and begged for him to snatch her up and whisk her to his den.

Frozen with shock, he could do nothing but stare.

Chapter 21

Ezmira

It was impossible to ignore the terror coursing through her veins, but it was even harder to ignore the feelings pulsing in her chest at the sight of her alpha. Music carried on the wind, and she had the oddest impulse to dance, but her feet stayed rooted in place.

Once Armyn realized what Quasim was likely planning, it hadn't taken long for them to get in the air. His sleek ship moved through the clouds without a sound, speeding them to the ruins of Cryptik. Ezmira had never had a chance to really see the destroyed city, and it was a shock to realize people were still living in such a ravaged place. It was hard to tell if war or time had destroyed what looked to have been a beautiful place, but she saw the similarities between her alpha and the derelict city.

It had taken longer to find a place for them to land the ship safely since Quasim's building had a domed roof and they were skeptical of its ability to hold the ship's weight. If it weren't for Armyn's wings, she never would have made it onto the balcony.

The trip had been the most terrifying moment of her life. Quasim would have heard her wails of terror had they not gotten trapped in her throat by the fear of slipping through Armyn's grasp. Even after her feet were firmly on the balcony, she'd kept her eyes clenched shut and couldn't force her body to move. The trembling wracking her left her heart fluttering in vain as her mind screamed to go inside.

But she hadn't had to take a step. Quasim had lurched onto the balcony, slamming the door into the wall behind him and causing her to jump, which released her frozen muscles.

"How..."

He trailed off, the confusion clear on his face. Ezmira forced a lungful of air into her chest as she let her eyes trail down to the bleeding mark she'd left on him.

"I-I had to come back."

It was hard to find her voice through everything swirling inside her, and she worried the wind had torn her whispered words away before they reached him. Swallowing, she forced herself to take a step closer, despite the weakness of her muscles.

"I couldn't leave you to—"

A sob cut off the thought before she could voice it, and she had to suck in another steadying breath.

"It's okay if you don't want to claim me. You-You don't have to do anything—"

The words caught in her throat again, fighting her as she stared at the man who'd somehow changed her entire life in just a few days. She knew it made little sense for her to feel so strongly for him when he'd done nothing more than small kindnesses after kidnapping her, but emotions didn't need explanation. They were there, and that was all that mattered.

"If you don't want me, I can leave. I can go far away, where you'll never see me again, and maybe the distance will lessen the—"

She was going to say pain but stopped herself. If anyone understood pain, it was the alpha standing before her.

Through everything she'd said, Quasim's eyes had stayed locked on hers. His expression changed from surprise to confusion, and she watched as rage slowly crept in. Swallowing her own surprise and the jolt of fear racing down her spine, she stood frozen in place as he moved, rushing forward to tower over her though he was careful to keep a breath of space between their bodies.

Despite the anger written on his features, it was all she could do not to lean into him. She wanted to melt against the warmth radiating from his skin, his scent rising to fill her head and distract her for a moment before his rough growl registered. Even then, her core clenched, reminding her that her cycle was not yet over.

"If I don't *want* you?"

His roar rang in her ears and made her flinch, shaking dirt from the wall behind him as it echoed between the buildings. When his voice dropped to a deadly, controlled rumble, she struggled to hear him over the drumming of her heart.

"I don't *want* you, little one. I *need* you. I crave you. My life means nothing without you, but I don't deserve you. You saved me from my agony, but all I've given you is pain and suffering. I was selfish, and I'm sorry. You don't deserve to be tied to a broken alpha."

His words lit a spark of hope inside her, even as the stark self-loathing in his tone made her ache to comfort him. Staring up into his grey eyes, she felt the turmoil inside him and the truth of his words. Everything he'd done after taking her, in his mind, had been done to protect her.

Quasim's chest heaved with his heavy breaths, the air trembling as he fought to control himself. She saw his muscles straining and the pain etched on his face, and she wanted nothing more than to soothe him and take that pain away.

"You're damaged. I understand that. But you're not broken."

Raising her hand, she cupped his cheek, a small smile lifting the corner of her mouth as he stilled. His lips popped open, but she continued before he could interrupt her.

"You are so strong. You've overcome the worst life could throw at you, and you still care."

Ezmira paused, thinking about what Armyn had told her on the flight to Cryptik. She'd suspected Quasim's injuries weren't from something as simple as an accident, and learning about the torture he'd suffered and the burden of guilt his friends bore for not saving him sooner had broken her heart. She'd never met another alpha who pulled at her the way Quasim did.

"I'm glad you took me. You woke me up from an existence I was dreading. You deserve so much more than I can offer you, but if I can do nothing more than bring you a moment's peace each day, then that is what I want to spend my days doing. Your friends want to help you too. Ursuli is still here, and he's willing to do what he can to improve your life."

Raising her other hand to cradle his face between her palms, she fought the need to press her lips to his. Being so close to him was bringing her heat back full force, and she was struggling not to kneel on the balcony and beg with her body instead of words.

"You've given me something I've been missing for so long without knowing what it was: A place to belong. A reason to feel again, and to fall back in love with dancing. If you want nothing more than to stay in this den and live out your days hidden away from the world, I'll stay here with you and dance your pain away for each one of them. When or if you're ever ready to rejoin the world, I'll follow you and stand proudly by your side."

Sniffling back the threatening tears, she let her hands drop to her sides and took a step back.

"Or if you only want to be left in peace, I'll go as far away as I can to be sure I don't cause you anymore suffering. But you must promise me you'll keep living. You're too strong to give up now."

Her eyes swam with unshed tears, blurring her view of Quasim as he continued to stand frozen before her. The longer it took him to respond, the more the fear inside her grew, but she steeled herself for his decision. She would honor whatever he chose.

She let out a gasp when he closed the space between them and swept her into his arms. Blinking to clear her sight, she stared up into his eyes, breath trapped in her chest as she waited.

"I can't live without you. I can't live knowing I'm causing you suffering."

His quiet words caused warmth to bloom in her chest, spreading until her entire body burned.

"Then claim me, Quasim. Make me yours, and I'll be by your side for the rest of our lives."

His lips covered hers before the last of her whisper faded away. Her eyes closed as she wrapped her arms around his neck, careful not to cause his injuries more pain. Losing herself in the feel of him, she barely noticed that he'd carried her inside, kicking the door shut behind him before striding across the room where she'd danced for him.

A spare thought flicked to Armyn waiting on the roof outside, prepared to intervene if she hadn't convinced Quasim not to do anything foolish, but her back hitting the mattress pulled all her focus to the male hovering over her. Hopefully, Armyn realized all was okay and left them alone until they were ready to reemerge. She had a mate to enjoy as he helped her through the end of her heat.

Lifting her hips from the bed, she helped Quasim pull her pants off before sitting up to tug the shirt over her head. The full force of her heat slammed into her as their mingled pheromones surrounded her. She was in no mood for taking their time. It seemed Quasim felt the same, because his pants hit the floor a moment later.

She didn't have time to admire him before he crawled over her, hands framing her face and pushing her hair out of the way.

"You're too good for me."

His quiet words held the edge of a growl, the pain behind them soul deep. She knew he wouldn't listen to her argument, so she said the first thing that popped into her mind.

"I'm good *for* you."

His rumble vibrated through her core as he pressed her down into the bed, her slick coating his stomach as he slid forward until his tip pressed to her entrance.

"Are you sure?"

Quasim had always sounded sure of himself, but in that moment, she knew he still fought the instinct to protect her, even from himself. He thought being bound to him would be a curse, but she knew it was a blessing in disguise. He was her home now, her anchor to keep her from drifting away like she'd done before he'd taken her for himself.

"Bite me, Quasim. No more questions."

With another growl, he surged into her. She arched her back and gasped. The way he filled her was glorious, the burning stretch adding an extra layer to the pleasure as he dragged his length out before burying it in her again.

She already felt the bulge of his knot swelling, tugging at her lower lips each time he pulled back. She whined and squirmed, trying to wriggle lower and trap the bulge inside her where it belonged.

"Please, Quasim," she begged.

Sitting up, his hands gripped her hips, tilting her so he could take her deeper. Harder. His ragged breaths told how close he was, each plunge into her core growing more difficult as his knot expanded. It wasn't long before it ballooned inside her; the first pulse of his hot seed sending her over the edge into bliss.

Ezmira cried out, eyes clamping shut as her orgasm rolled through her. Still rocking his hips as much as he could, Quasim ground against her, sending her higher and higher until her vision went white.

His grip shifted behind her back, pulling her until her chest pressed against his. Nuzzling the side of her neck, he licked her sweaty skin before his lips trailed down to where it met her shoulder.

"Mine."

The snarl sent goosebumps down her arms before Quasim filled his mouth with her flesh and bit. The spark of pain morphed to pleasure, shooting straight to her core and pulling another orgasm from her.

His teeth stayed locked in her as his cock kicked again, spilling more of his seed deep inside. The twisted pressure in her chest released, the bond snapping into place between them and filling her with awe as the depths of his emotions flooded through her. There was pain, more pain than she'd ever imagined, and she pulled as much to her as she could, tucking it away and focusing on the better things.

The awe. The comfort. The love.

A sigh slipped from her as his jaw released, his tongue swiping over the wound to seal it. Her body sagged, the energy draining from her while her mind still wondered at the man who'd given her his soul.

Turning so he could lean against the bedpost with her draped over his lap, Quasim cupped her cheek and pulled her gaze up to his.

"Are you okay?"

Instead of answering in words, she sent a pulse of her feelings along their bond, watching his eyes widen in surprise before his lips tipped up in the corner. It was the first time she'd ever seen him smile, and she pushed her happiness into him, trying to encourage it to grow.

Stroking her hair and brushing her antlers with his other hand, he pulled her head to his chest, a gentle purr vibrating into her ear. She rubbed her cheek against the downy feathers, the scars beneath them only adding to the sensation.

She knew Quasim was still going to struggle with his demons, what he'd suffered wasn't something he would ever forget, but she'd told the truth out on the balcony, and if he wanted to stay hidden away in this den forever, she'd remain by his side.

Chapter 22

Quasim

His heart jumped into his throat as Ezmira popped upright and turned wide eyes to him. His knot shifted inside her, making them both moan in pleasure before she regained her senses.

"You're bleeding! Where are—"

The panic in her voice snapped into him from their bond, but her emotions changed as her eyes zeroed in on the mark she'd left on his chest.

"Oh, Quasim. I'm sorry."

Tears gathered in her eyes. He hated them, so he snarled and filled his grip with her hair.

"Don't apologize. I've had worse."

His words only made her sadder, but he felt her pull her emotions away from him, which enraged him further. After an embarrassing fumble, he snatched her retreating sorrow and yanked it closer.

"I didn't understand how deep the bond would reach, but now that I have you, I never want distance between us again. Don't hide from me, Ezmira."

She searched his eyes before nodding. Her fingers trailed up his chest until she circled the partially healed mark. After an audible swallow, she met his gaze and firmed her resolve.

"Will you let me clean it so I can lick it again?"

Quasim's fingers loosened in her hair and stroked the silky locks. The lump in his throat stopped him from speaking, so he nodded his head before a smirk pulled on the scarred flesh on the side of his face.

"After I lick you clean."

Her cheeks flushed, the midnight tint of her skin gaining a gorgeous pink, and he purred as her insides tightened around him.

"Quasim, that's... if that's what you want?"

He studied her face before rubbing his knuckles along her cheekbone.

"I need to, my prize. Has no one ever tended you properly after your heats?"

One dainty brow lifted as she shuddered around his knot even though he hadn't moved, but her expression softened, and she shook her head.

"The alphas in my troupe were always careful. They didn't want a mate, just like they didn't want to settle in one place, so they always left as soon as they knew my heat was over."

Quasim growled in indignation and nuzzled her head.

"I want every part of you, Ezmira. With you, I have no control. No limits. You've pulled my broken pieces back together and fused them with your soul. I'm free to trust my instincts again. Let me treat you like the prize you are. Let me show you how an alpha worships his omega."

After an uneven inhale, she nodded against his chest and eased her arms around his waist.

It might be a while before he could show her how attentive his tongue could be since the fluttering of her womb kept stealing more seed from him and, therefore, kept his knot fully inflated. Even though he knew she loved his invasion, he also felt her troubled emotions, so he urged her to settle against him. Quasim stroked her back and purred, digging his spine into the bedpost in hopes the pain would expedite the deflation of his knot.

Time passed, neither one keeping track of how much as they relaxed into their new reality. Her purr joined his rumble as she faded into a soft, contented doze, and he rested his cheek on the top of her head, careful not to hurt her antlers.

Whether he followed her into a light sleep or found a peace so profound he couldn't move, Quasim couldn't tell, but the pop of his knot slipping loose and a gush of hot liquid surprised him into motion.

He pushed her onto her back and grabbed the underside of her knees, pressing them to her shoulders as he delved between her legs. His mouth latched onto her folds, halting the flow of fluids as he eagerly gobbled up what he could.

Her moan joined his purr.

Quasim let go of her legs, worrying he'd been too rough, but Ezmira's fingers slid against his scalp almost tentatively as she filled their bond with her enjoyment. He tried to gentle his tongue, but it kept lapping at her as his instincts demanded he claim every drop of their essences.

When he'd licked her folds clean, he trailed down her legs until she made a disgruntled sound.

He looked up at her body with a creased brow.

"I... I want to taste you too."

His purr deepened until her pupils lost their focus, the pleasure flowing between them so intense, the tension left her.

Sitting back on his heels, Quasim offered Ezmira his hand. When she took it without hesitation, wonder filled his heart.

He helped her sit up, tucking her hair behind her ear before putting his palms on his thighs, letting her approach him at her own pace. She glanced at his face, trailed her fingers across the scars on the back of his hand, then dropped her gaze to his cock.

The same instincts that had ruled him when he'd licked her clean took hold of her. Ezmira lowered her forearms to the bed between his thighs, graceful even then, and licked the underside of his cock from base to tip.

Quasim growled as euphoria swept through him. It took every ounce of control he possessed to dig his fingers into his thighs and give her the freedom to care for him the way her omega instincts demanded. By the time she'd run her soft tongue all around him, his jaw felt as though it would burst from the grinding of his teeth.

She stole a groan from him as she wrapped her lips around the sensitive, flanged ring of his head. Three bobs of her mouth later, and he wrapped his fist in her hair and pulled her away.

Quasim framed her face and brought her lips to his, nipping her bottom lip before worshipping her with a soft yet deep kiss.

When he pulled away, they both breathed heavily.

"Thank you, my prize. Anymore, and I'll knot you again."

A small smile tugged her lips up, but her fingers brushed against the sticky trail on his pectoral and her expression tightened.

Sensing her need to care for his bite mark, he let her stand, but when she stepped toward the bathroom, he grabbed her hand and rose from the bed. His knee bones ground together as usual, but with her light pouring into him, he didn't have to grit his teeth.

When he stepped in front to lead her to the washroom, her hiss made him spin around in search of an enemy.

"Why is your back bleeding?"

Quasim pulled her to him and cocooned her in his arms. He refused to tell her it was because he'd used a harness to carry her. She'd blame herself, and he hated the thought.

"It happens sometimes when I overdo it. It's fine."

"No, it isn't."

She caressed his arm and took a deep inhale, then started toward the bathroom.

His purr rumbled from him, her fierce protectiveness over him a balm he never knew he needed. She led him past the curtain and stepped into the bathing room, only to stop and stare at the mess.

The poor excuse for bedding floated in the old bath water, and he'd left hangers strewn over the floor from when he'd emptied his closet for her nest. Before he could bend to pick the closest hanger up, she tightened her grip around his wrist.

With a motion toward the bath and a silent plea within their bond, she effectively sent him to do her bidding. While he turned on the water heater and let the bath drain, she gathered the hangers and put them back in their place. After filling the tub with hot water, he stooped to grab the nearest blanket but stopped in his tracks when a feminine growl rolled through the room.

"You're making it worse. Stop bending. Every time you do, your back bleeds. Let me clean and bandage it before you agitate it further."

Quasim slowly turned to meet her gaze over his left shoulder.

She tried to appear calm, but her need to care for him burned in their bond. The fury shining from her vibrant green eyes took his breath away. He stood and faced her, loving how cute she looked with her locks tangled in her antlers from their mating. Her hourglass shape and fierce expression made him want to sink into her depths.

"If you think I'm going to stand here and watch as you wash laundry while I do nothing, then keep being angry, my prize. I will happily pin you against the tub and mount you from behind. Every drop of blood I lose will be worth it, especially if you'll turn those fiery eyes on me again."

Her mouth popped open and her breathing quickened, even as she scrunched her nose in consternation.

"Please let me bandage it."

He melted. Everything inside him turned to mush as she pierced him with wide, shimmery emerald eyes.

Unable to bear the distance between them, he gathered her close and kissed the top of her head, brushing his unmarred cheek against her fuzzy antlers, trying to keep his cock from hardening against her. The attempt failed, and her purr joined his as bare flesh slid together.

This mated thing was so complex. They had so much to figure out.

Her need to care for him pulsed along their connection, so he relented.

She kissed his bicep, stepping out of his arms to pluck a washcloth from the bath and lather it with soap. With soft touches, she positioned him to sit on the edge of the tub.

The sound of water splashing mingled with their purrs as she gently washed the torn skin over his right shoulder. She moved in front of him and stepped between his spread legs, blushing as the underside of his hard shaft brushed along her stomach. A few seconds later, after she'd washed the bite mark on his chest, she reached around him and plopped the cloth back into the bath.

"Where are the bandages?"

He wanted to argue and say he didn't need any, but the look in her eyes stopped him.

"In the chest by the door. It's unlocked."

Ezmira kissed his chest and murmured for him to stay where he was. She disappeared into the other room before returning with two handfuls of supplies. After rubbing ointment on the cracked skin of his back, she taped gauze over it and pressed little reverent closed-mouth kisses all around the edges.

He longed to weep over her sweetness but transferred the emotion into a purr instead.

"Quasim?"

He hummed an appropriate note, letting her know he was listening.

"Will you let Ursuli help? At least let him look at your injuries?"

He stopped purring and swallowed, every muscle in his body tensed. When he didn't respond, Ezmira rested her cheek on his shoulder and whispered her next words.

"I just don't want you to hurt so much. If he can ease your pain, even the smallest amount, I think we should at least try."

A single tear dripped onto his arm, even as she tried to hide her worry from him. Instead of spiraling into his normal self-hatred, his heart shook in wonder.

"Then we'll visit Ursuli."

Happiness filled his heart as her infectious joy swept through him. She slid around him and graced him with a smile before gently placing her hand on his abdominals.

Who knew an alpha could turn to jelly and yet be rock hard at the same time?

She trailed her palm up his sternum until it reached the level of her claiming mark, then tucked her bottom lip between her teeth and searched his expression. Quasim grabbed her hips and pulled her against him as she glanced at the mark she'd left on his chest. Her eyebrows drew together before she looked back up at him. Without saying a word, Ezmira stretched and ran her tongue over the entire wound.

Stars exploded behind his eyes as pleasure flooded their bond. Needing her more than his next breath, he grabbed her and spun around.

He had an omega to please and a tub that was the perfect height.

***

Quasim finished stoking the fire and limped back to the bed. Ezmira looked up from her newly made nest and reached for him. He let her guide him down onto the fabric, vowing to get her the best nesting materials on the planet, no matter what it took.

A pop sounded from the roaring fire, making Quasim snarl and pull Ezmira closer to him. Her hum of delight demanded his attention, and when he met her eyes, he reveled in the satisfaction glowing from them.

"I enjoy knowing you're ready to protect me."

"Anything to keep you safe."

Despite having knotted her twice in the last few hours, he wanted nothing more than to sink into her again. Ezmira framed his face with delicate hands and tugged him closer. He aimed for her mouth but teased them both by merely brushing his closed lips against hers.

Even as she whimpered for more, her body relaxed into the nest.

Quasim pulled his lips away and tugged her against his chest.

"You need rest, not another knotting. Go to sleep."

"I don't want sleep. I want more of you."

Her pretty words made him smile, but Ezmira's eyes had already closed as she edged toward slumber.

The top log shifted in the fireplace, and Quasim swore as he jostled his exhausted omega.

"Why are you so jumpy?"

Her slurred words made him scowl. He did not know why he was overreacting.

The telltale crack of a door banging open had him bolting from the bed and realizing why his instincts were on high alert—someone lurked around his sanctuary.

He tossed Ezmira her clothes and yanked his pants up his legs, uncaring when his talon ripped another hole in them.

Ezmira's wide, startled eyes searched his as she settled her shirt over her shoulders.

"It's probably Armyn?"

Her shaky voice held hope, but he refused to let his guard down in case it wasn't his friend.

"Stay right behind me."

Quasim reached deep into the bottom of the chest and pulled out two knives, stacking them in one hand while he unlocked the door. He motioned for Ezmira to stay a few feet back while he checked the hall. When he didn't see anyone, he urged her closer before shifting a knife to each hand.

His talons scraped across the floor despite his attempt at stealth since his knee refused to cooperate, but he moved forward with as much caution as he could.

Rage boiled in his bones, the threat to his omega making him want to rampage and slay whatever enemy dared enter their sanctuary, but her fear stopped him from rushing forward. She followed a step behind him, her unease buffeting their bond despite her obvious attempt to hold it back from him.

His anger grew and preceded them down the short hall until he'd already imagined covering the ballroom with the blood of his enemies a million times before he stepped foot into the room. Three alphas stood on the other side of the space, not quite halfway across the dance floor. His muscles bunched for a fight until their scents broke through his adrenaline.

The alphas he'd gone to war with faced him as a unit. His brothers were here, together, to check on him. After he'd pulled away despite their attempts to help him, they still had his back.

Or they were trying to be sure he hadn't completely lost his shit and turned on his precious omega—no matter how brutal they'd been in the past, his team had always done everything they could to protect innocents.

Armyn's bright blue wings relaxed as his golden eyes perused Quasim. He shifted his weight backward in a move to show he would not attack. To his right stood a large furry beast, the dark mantle that was Blaide's coat making him almost invisible in the dim morning light. On Armyn's other side, only Ursuli's electric yellow eyes and grey hair shone from the darkness.

Quasim had seen them at Armyn's homecoming ball a few days ago, that fateful night when he'd kidnapped Ezmira, but he'd purposefully kept his distance. He'd missed them but didn't want to infect their lives.

They each met his eyes before Armyn did what he did best. He took charge.

"Good to see she talked some sense into you," Armyn said.

Blaide slid into his role of a jester with ease and quipped, "I doubt they did much talking."

Armyn threw his head back and laughed.

"Don't encourage him. Wouldn't want him to get a big head. Careful, pup, or you might find your tail in trouble."

The words tumbled from Quasim's mouth as though he were back in the barracks with them so many years ago, joking around on a rare day off. His body hurt, but bittersweet memories flowed through him. The parts of himself he'd buried during the worst of times bloomed to life, aided by the sweet omega standing behind him.

He shuffled around and offered her his hand. Her gorgeous green irises shone in the growing light as the sun rose above the surrounding buildings.

"Ezmira, you've met Armyn. Meet Blaide and Ursuli."

Quasim motioned to each alpha as he wrapped his left arm around her waist and tugged her to his side. She came to him but didn't relax.

"Thank you, Prince Armyn, for bringing me back."

Realization dawned inside him, just like the sun, and he saw his brothers from her perspective. She was tiny compared to him, which meant each of his buddies towered over her as well, and they oozed lethal power. He understood why she stood rigid, but it didn't mean he had to like it.

Quasim stroked her arm and rumbled a purr. He trusted these men with his life, and even his omega's life, if the situation demanded it.

"Just call me Armyn. The mate of my longest and dearest friend doesn't owe me such formality."

Ursuli's smooth voice followed as he spoke for the first time, still as sharp as ever.

"My Arana really ripped you to shreds, didn't she, Armyn? Cinza no doubt knocked you down a peg or two as well. Thank the universe for feisty omegas, otherwise you'd still have your ass glued to that hoity-toity throne twenty-four seven."

"And you'd still be living in a cave," Armyn shot back.

More stress eased from him as his brothers continued their ribbing, which loosened the stiffness in Ezmira's muscles.

Quasim looked down past her adorable antlers and vibrant hair and met her gaze, the moment too perfect for him to look elsewhere. He wanted to watch her dance again, not so she could take his pain away, but because he longed to connect with her in that all-consuming way again.

A faint smile ghosted across her lips before her expression sobered.

"Ursuli is here."

He smiled and stroked her hair, unable to deny himself the pleasure of her silky tresses, before nodding and turning his attention to Ursuli.

"Is that offer of help still available?"

A beam of sunlight shone through a broken windowpane and glinted off the stained glass, revealing Ursuli's solid black frame and the matching tendrils of smoke wrapping around his legs.

"Always, my brother."

Epilogue

Quasim

Quasim grinned as Ezmira offered him her hand. Her dark skin bore a flush from her energetic dance, and many eyes still lingered on her. He wanted to whisk her away and hide her from her adoring fans so he could have her all to himself, but he also enjoyed knowing she'd awed the crowd.

When Armyn had formally requested her to perform at his coronation ball, Ezmira had looked at him with a torn expression. She didn't want to share what had become an intimate thing with so many people, but Quasim couldn't let her pass up the opportunity. She'd forever worry about letting down his friend.

As Ezmira led him onto the dance floor, a song began, the tune known by all in attendance. Sung to younglings for generations, Ezmira changed the meaning of the simple melody as she wrapped her arms around him. She hugged him close, claiming him with the action, so the masses understood who held her heart.

After straightening, she fixed his vest and held her arms up in expectation. He took her hands, still hesitant as he raised his right arm higher than he had in months. Ursuli had worked magic and eased the knotted muscles surrounding his injuries after removing the broken stumps sticking out from his flesh. He still had pain and joked about forever being hunchback, but it was nothing like the agony he'd suffered before.

Unable to resist Ezmira's infectious joy, he smirked down at her as he began the simple dance she'd taught him. The skin on his head pulled significantly less with the movement, but he'd never regain his hearing or be scar-free. He found himself not caring, since he could feel his mate's acceptance of him as he was.

They'd spent two months together, but not once had she ever shown signs of reticence or regret. She'd burst through his defenses with her colorful skirts and gathered his pieces and filled his future with hope.

Green hair fanned out around her as he twirled her, and when she settled back into position, he swooped down and claimed her mouth.

She awed him.

Three nights after their initial mating, he'd woken from a horrible nightmare, ready to tear apart his enemies. Before his eyes had even popped open, her purr had invaded his heart. He'd refrained from attacking. The knowledge that he could have hurt her shook him, but she'd reassured him before distracting him with her tempting body.

Her ability to handle his mood swings was so graceful, he likened it to her dancing.

The pink on her cheeks as he pulled away held more than just a flush from her spirited dance, and he tightened his grip on her hands. Quasim straightened his spine, standing taller since Ursuli had thinned the scar tissue and smoothed the torn flesh around his missing wings. They danced across the invisible square of floor they'd staked as theirs for the dance as the crowd joined in around them.

Life would never be easy, but with Ezmira in his arms, Quasim would live it to the fullest. He had something to look forward to again, besides a life of misery and pain.

And if he whisked her off the dance floor as soon as the song ended and carried her up to the bedroom, it was because he couldn't wait a second longer to do exactly what he planned to do for the rest of their lives.

Love Ezmira.

Join V.T. Bonds' newsletter for a STEAMY BONUS SCENE of Ezmira and Quasim!

Author's Note

Since neither of us have ever cowritten a story before (yes, we wrote this before Rescuing Red), we must admit these characters hold special places in our hearts. They helped us learn so much together, and now that we've shared them with you, we can't help but express our gratitude. If this is your first read from either of us, we hope we've intrigued you enough to seek more from both Leann Ryans and V.T. Bonds. If you're one of our established fans, then hopefully you'll see the unique touch we each brought to the world.

Are you ready for more? Because we are. Always ready to delve into the next steamy, knotty romance novel. We welcome all devious and depraved souls.

Forever thankful,
Leann Ryans and V.T. Bonds

Unknown Omega

Alpha Elite Series Book 1

V.T. Bonds

Unknown Omega by V.T. Bonds (Preview)

Seeck

A streak of dark brown curls flies past the mouth of the alley. The blur of her shape rocketing across gives the distinct impression that she's running for her life.

Then her smell hits me. Rich, beautiful, and wrong. A confusing mixture of incompleteness. She should be beta, but she smells of omega.

And blood. I smell the metallic scent and can't stop my body from reacting. My cock grows stiff even as my instincts demand I protect her.

There's the distinct smell of her blood, a puzzle of beauty and pain, and a male's musk clinging to her. His blood mingles with a delicate, specific kind of scent and my body moves of its own accord. The smell of her broken innocence strips all conscious thought from me.

I hurtle up the wall of the decrepit building and launch myself onto the roof. Sprinting, decreasing the space between us, I run over the crumbling structure.

I fling myself over the edge, and the sand buffets my landing. A need fiercer than any rut overwhelms me, so strong that I don't care about my lack of control.

Reaching the front of the alley, I extend my arm and brace for impact.

She runs straight into it, but she's so small that I barely register the hit.

I snatch her out of the air, surrounding her with my arms, clutching her to my chest.

Before she can regain her breath, I drag her deeper into the narrow passage. My hand clamps over her mouth and chin.

Having her so close shreds my hold on reality. Seeing the wild array of hair short circuits my thoughts. Smelling her body and pain within my arms causes a well of need to burst inside me.

I push her against the wall and her cry of pain and fright dampens my need a bit. I meet her eyes and the world shifts.

Everything makes sense. She's mine. My own. My other half. My Omega. My weakness.

Continue reading *Unknown Omega (Alpha Elite Series Book 1)* direct from V.T. Bonds' website for an exclusive discount:

https://vtbonds.com/product/unknownomega/

Monster's Find

Monsters in the Mountains Book 1

LEANN RYANS

Monster's Find by Leann Ryans (Preview)

Sasha

"Don't let me interrupt you, little omega. I was enjoying the show." The gruff voice echoed through the darkness, ripping a gasp from me as I scrambled to my belly and backed away from the sound. My entire body throbbed with denied need as I crouched and tried desperately to see the source. A small part of my brain recognized I was in danger, but my body's response was to release more slick to coat my thighs.

Like that would save me.

The next cramp threatened to tear my body in half, pulling my focus back to myself as the muscles in my middle rippled and forced me into a ball of misery at the edge of my pitiful nest. Whoever had spoken wasn't someone I recognized, and I was beyond the point of being able to run.

"Please..."

It was the only word I could force past trembling lips, and even I didn't know what I was asking for. Part of me demanded I send the male away, while another part wanted me to present and beg him for relief. The deepness of the voice and the scent surrounding me left no question the speaker was an alpha, and it didn't matter that he was a stranger.

I *needed*.

"Please what, little one? Are you in distress?"

A whimper was my only response. With the pheromones of the male taking effect in my brain, the cramps became nonstop, one rolling in on the heels of the last, leaving me breathless and crying into the thin grass covering the stone. My core clenched over and over, demanding to be filled with thick alpha cock.

The same scraping sound I'd heard before came closer, stopping at the edge of the little depression I'd claimed for my nest. A low growl left my throat before I could stop it, but it was met with a chuckle from the hulking male I sensed just outside my temporary bed.

"Temper, temper! I'm only offering to give you what you want."

There was a strange accent to the words the male spoke, but they were clear enough to understand. Despite the delicious scent rolling off him and the demands of my body, it was instinct to protect my nest, even as pitiful as it was, until the alpha proved himself.

There still wasn't any light in the cave, but the male's presence was enough for my eyes to lock on to where I assumed he stood. A sense of motion caused me to flinch further away, but there were no more scraping footsteps, and nothing touched me.

He waited.

Another harsh cramp broke my focus again, the desire between my thighs growing more desperate with each breath filled with the male's musk. My hand slipped to my core without conscious thought, two fingers dipping into my entrance to ease the pain but only succeeding in making me more miserable.

It wasn't enough. I needed more.

I couldn't last through days of this. It was torture. I was going to die in misery.

I pushed another finger into my opening, ignoring the alpha's presence as I thrust in and out with desperation. The wet sounds would have embarrassed me at any other time, but they barely registered as my world narrowed to the tension coiled through my belly. Something had to give, and I was scared it would be me, giving in to the male lurking so close.

A soft moan escaped my throat as my knuckles stretched my entrance, but it still wasn't enough. My fingers were too short. Too thin.

"Poor omega. I have what your body craves, if only you'd let me into your nest."

I snarled toward the male, turning my back to where the voice originated. It came from lower than it had before, and I could picture him crouching on the edge of my nest, watching as I tried to ease the ache.

Waiting for the inevitable.

His scent was divine. There was a saltiness to it now that spoke of virility. That called to the animal part of me and told me this was a male in his prime.

A male worth submitting to.

I panted as my fingers worked, wrist starting to ache. Free hand braced against the stone edge of my wallow, I rode my thrusting digits, but it couldn't provide the stretch or the friction my nature demanded. Even adding my little finger to the other three did nothing.

I needed a knot.

Time had no meaning in the desperate daze I'd fallen into. It could have been hours, or days, or mere breaths that passed in my search for relief before I finally collapsed with a sob, my hand stilling. I'd almost forgotten about the male perched at the side of my nest until he spoke again.

"Give in, little one. Let me soothe your pain."

"I will submit to no man."

My hiss was weak, mocking as it echoed back to me even as a chuckle rumbled overtop it.

"Well, *I* am no *man*."

Continue reading *Monster's Find (Monsters in the Mountains Book 1)* by Leann Ryans:

https://books2read.com/monsters-find-1

Rescued and Ruined

Warrior Elite Series Book 1

V.T. Bonds

Rescued and Ruined by V.T. Bonds (Preview)

Craize

Something calls me. Blood rains down the walls. Crimson colors the ceiling.

I sink into a rage just as potent as what I felt as I watched my race being caught. A fury as explosive as the anger I felt upon hearing they were experimented on and slaughtered in the most disgusting ways possible.

My shriveled soul expands, seeking the source of whatever beckons me.

The weight of mountains presses down on the ceiling, every step deeper into the facility adding to the oppressive sense of claustrophobia. Not caring whether my teammates follow on my heels or turn to find relief in the sky, I murder any individual in my path. When a large, circular concrete door blocks my path, a roar bursts from my chest, making the fluorescent lights shake within their moors. I crank the lever and rip the offending material from its hinges and toss it away, snarling as the ground beneath me vibrates with its landing.

The hall beyond lacks the stark lighting of those behind me, even the red emergency lights bright compared to the ones below. Ominous dread wafts up from the tunnel, carrying scents of despair and death.

I cross the threshold, my hope dead long ago, my life ruled by hatred and pain. My salvation lies within this darkness. It shrieks in misery, begging me to end its suffering.

Ignoring the doors lining the hall, I continue into the bowels of hell, prepared to desecrate any monsters residing within such an abhorrent place. I follow my screaming instincts, the invisible lead yanking me toward the last door on the left.

It bursts inward in shards of metal and wood, my boot cracking it down the middle. The two ends warp the doorway, the right half tilting and falling as the lock snaps under the weight while the left swings on precarious hinges.

Jumping through the wrecked vestibule long before the last of the fragments hit the once-smooth flooring, my hackles rise as the most feral snarl rips through the air. It isn't until the cloud of debris almost settles that I realize the ache in my throat is from creating the animalistic sound, but my logical mind stands no chance against the need to find whatever lured me here.

Ugly brown orbs appear out of the dust, a human male baring his puny teeth at me in challenge. His dark clothing hides most of his form, but a triangle reveals his jutting cock, the tip spurting acrid liquid.

As he swings his fist despite his eyes popping wide in terror, I grab the sides of his head and slam my forehead down on his.

Gore squishes between us as the pattern of short horns on my forehead embed themselves into his skull, their jagged edges sliding through his bone as though it were butter. I avoid the putrid liquid leaking from his manhood but glory in shedding his lifeblood, jerking my head back and watching as crimson paints his face.

His fist thumps against my side even as his legs begin to crumple. I grab his neck and squeeze, adding another hand and wrenching his trachea.

He thumps to the ground, his neck at an odd angle and his eyes clouding over.

Movement and sounds of struggle break my satisfied stare, and the agony in my chest pulls me further into the room.

A tiny form contorts on a filthy mattress, her white flesh blending into its surroundings despite her vicious lurching.

I step closer, my senses zeroing in on the figure, the pull behind my sternum demanding I reach her. Pert breasts wobble and trim legs create the most luscious form I've ever seen, and even as my conscience screams within my hijacked mind, basal needs demand I take. Claim. Own.

I stalk forward and pin a slim ankle to the mattress.

Bright green irises pierce mine, abject misery shining from a face too delicate for words.

She's the reason I'm here. She called me.

Somehow, she reached into my soul and beckoned me into the pits of hell.

She's *mine*.

Continue reading *Rescued and Ruined (Warrior Elite Series Book 1)* direct from V.T. Bonds' website for an exclusive discount:

https://vtbonds.com/product/rescuedandruined/

TEMPTING A KNIGHT

Hell's Knights MC Book 1

LEANN RYANS

Tempting A Knight by Leann Ryans (Preview)

Brooke

I needed help.

I bit my lower lip to stop it from trembling. Blinking back tears, I dropped my gaze to the stained concrete, trying to come up with something to convince Sebastian to agree. This was the only plan that had a chance of working.

Before I could think of a valid argument, a large hand landed on my shoulder, startling a small yelp from my throat before I could choke it back. Spun around to face the open garage doors, I was thrust forward by the hard grip.

Chuckles followed as Sebastian marched me out of his garage. The size of it proved how well the business had done, and it provided a place for his motorcycle club to hang out during the day. I didn't know much about the Hell's Knights, but they were discussed in whispers just as much as the Purists. The main difference was that Sebastian's club was more inclusive and respected by the average person, while the Purists were hated except by sympathizers.

Sebastian didn't release my shoulder until I cleared the building, and I took two more steps before turning to face him again once he let me go. His ridicule would be better than what I'd face with Arik if I didn't find a way out of his reach.

"Please."

The whisper was pathetic, and shame burned my cheeks as I resorted to begging.

Omegas were desired, shifter or not. They bore whatever they mated with, so there was plenty of interbreeding. I should have had alphas fighting over me, not be forced to beg one to take pity on me and see me through my heat to save me from another.

The problem was finding someone who didn't answer to the Purists, wouldn't claim me, and wouldn't enjoy hurting me.

Movement to the right caught my attention but I ignored it to keep my gaze locked on the man in front of me. Even if they were Knights and a better choice than Arik, the others weren't who I was here for. It was hard enough to place my trust in a man I barely knew, but my brother had trusted Sebastian.

"Just for this cycle. I'll figure out something else before the next. I'm not asking you to claim me or do anything more. It's just a couple days."

Sebastian's eyes narrowed, his features hardening, but he remained silent. The figure who'd approached from the side stepped into my field of vision, another grease-stained alpha, though smaller than Sebastian. His stringy hair was slicked back from a narrow face, his grin sporting missing teeth despite being around my age.

"I'll tend you through your heat, pretty. You say when and where, and my knot is yours."

A shudder rolled down my spine at his leer, the way his eyes focused on my breasts as he adjusted his crotch making my stomach surge. The scent of something wet and dirty rolled off him, gagging me further. I parted my lips to form a denial, but a harsh growl rumbled through the air before the words could emerge from my throat.

Hands clutching my belly as it spasmed, I fought to stay upright under the weight of an alpha's displeasure. As civilized as people tried to pretend they were, we were still animals at our core, and instincts were impossible to ignore.

There were different kinds of growls, but this one was clearly full of rage, and it took a moment before I realized it came from Sebastian but wasn't aimed at me.

Dark eyes locked on the second male, lips pulled back in a snarl as his canines elongated, the noise continued until the other alpha bowed his head and backed away, apology lost under the grating noise assaulting my nerves. Trembling, I stared at the ground and sucked in great gasps of air when it finally faded away, drenched in sweat and on the verge of tears.

I didn't notice Sebastian move closer until his boots appeared on the concrete in front of me. Dragging my gaze up his body until my head tipped back, I was hit once again with how large he was. Human alphas were big, but shifter alphas tended to be even more massive.

Unlike the other male who'd approached, Sebastian's scent wasn't revolting. It wrapped around me, filling my lungs with each inhale and making my eyes want to roll back in my head as I shuddered.

The omega part of me knew this was a strong, dominant male and was ready to roll over and present for him at the first sign of acceptance. The wholly female part enjoyed all that was before me. He was everything an alpha should be. Everything

I desired rolled into one delicious package that I shouldn't want beyond what I needed him for.

"Go home, Brooke, this isn't the place for you. You're better than this. Vincent would be disappointed."

Continue reading *Tempting A Knight (Hell's Knights MC Book 1)* by Leann Ryans:

https://books2read.com/tempting-a-knight

Follow V.T. Bonds

V.T. Bonds is a two-time USA Today Bestselling Author of dark and dirty contemporary, paranormal, and sci-fi romance. As a female veteran and mom of five kids, she enjoys writing filthy, action-packed romances with strong females and possessive alphas.

Go to https://vtbonds.com for a complete list of books by V.T. Bonds.

For new releases, discounts, and Knotty Exclusives, subscribe to V.T. Bonds' newsletter at https://vtbonds.com/newslettersubscriber.

***

Other places to follow V.T. Bonds:

Bookbub

Goodreads

Facebook

***

Embrace the dark, filthy side of omegaverse.

Brought to you by V.T. Bonds, The Knottiverse is a universe full of nesting, knots, morally grey alphas, and omegas who become the center of their mate's world.

Guaranteed to leave you slick, each story contains an HEA and at least one larger-than-life alpha.

Enter The Knottiverse now at:

https://vtbonds.com/the-knottiverse/

Follow Leann Ryans

I'm a wife and mother of four who's been an avid reader since I could pick up a book. It wasn't unusual for me to read a book a day, ignoring the real world as I was sucked into the pages of a great story.

I grew up on sci-fi and fantasy books before discovering the world of romance. PNR has always been my go-to, and omegaverse is my addiction of choice.

I love writing books featuring heroes who are a bit rough around the edges but aren't overly cruel. My heroines aren't always the take charge type, but neither are all women. They are comfortable in their femininity.

If you're looking for a story that has dark themes without leaving you wanting to punch the hero in the face, mine just might be for you.

***

To see Leann Ryans' full catalog, including books not available on all retailers, check out https://leannryans.com.